## They were outnumbered

The inspector's hand shot under his coat for the gun in his shoulder holster. Immediately, Bolan covered the man's arm with his left palm and pinned it. In the split second the man tried to yank his weapon free, the Executioner's right hand rose like a blunt ax and swept down, shattering his collarbone. The man screamed as he fell to the floor.

"Gun!"

Bolan recognized Dr. Lopez's voice. Then he saw the Skorpion machine pistol. He had been on the wrong end of such assassination weapons more times than he cared to recall. Bolan took the only course available.

He leaped at the gun.

The bullets tore through Bolan's coat and slammed into his stomach.

D1115232

# MACK BOLAN®
## The Executioner

# DON PENDLETON'S
# THE EXECUTIONER®
## CHILL EFFECT

## A GOLD EAGLE BOOK FROM
# WORLDWIDE®

TORONTO • NEW YORK • LONDON
AMSTERDAM • PARIS • SYDNEY • HAMBURG
STOCKHOLM • ATHENS • TOKYO • MILAN
MADRID • WARSAW • BUDAPEST • AUCKLAND

First edition January 2000
ISBN 0-373-64254-7

Special thanks and acknowledgment to
Chuck Rogers for his contribution to this work.

CHILL EFFECT

Printed in U.S.A.

One who deceives will always find those who allow
themselves to be deceived.

—Niccolo Machiavelli
*The Prince*

It was beautiful and simple as all truly great swindles are.

—O. Henry

I will never allow the rich and powerful to manipulate
the government for their selfish gains.

—Mack Bolan

# THE
# MACK BOLAN®
## LEGEND

Nothing less than a war could have fashioned the destiny of the man called Mack Bolan. Bolan earned the Executioner title in the jungle hell of Vietnam.

But this soldier also wore another name—Sergeant Mercy. He was so tagged because of the compassion he showed to wounded comrades-in-arms and Vietnamese civilians.

Mack Bolan's second tour of duty ended prematurely when he was given emergency leave to return home and bury his family, victims of the Mob. Then he declared a one-man war against the Mafia.

He confronted the Families head-on from coast to coast, and soon a hope of victory began to appear. But Bolan had broken society's every rule. That same society started gunning for this elusive warrior—to no avail.

So Bolan was offered amnesty to work within the system against terrorism. This time, as an employee of Uncle Sam, Bolan became Colonel John Phoenix. With a command center at Stony Man Farm in Virginia, he and his new allies—Able Team and Phoenix Force—waged relentless war on a new adversary: the KGB.

But when his one true love, April Rose, died at the hands of the Soviet terror machine, Bolan severed all ties with Establishment authority.

Now, after a lengthy lone-wolf struggle and much soul-searching, the Executioner has agreed to enter an "arm's-length" alliance with his government once more, reserving the right to pursue personal missions in his Everlasting War.

# PROLOGUE

*London, England*

The assassin raised an eyebrow as the British Foreign Secretary regarded his Argentine counterpart. "Then, please tell me, Señor Obradors, what possible purpose could the Argentine government have in acquiring surplus American 637 Sturgeon-class nuclear attack submarines other than with an eye toward reclaiming the Falkland Islands?"

The assassin took a sip of champagne and turned to gaze upon the Argentine ambassador. The killer nodded sympathetically as the South American statesman spoke with growing passion. "That's ridiculous! My government has no interest in the Falkland Islands! That foolishness occurred nearly twenty years ago, and you know as well as I do that unfortunate debacle was the desperate gamble of a corrupt and failing military dictatorship. The government of Argentina has been democratically elected ever since the end of that conflict and the fall of the military government. The vast majority of our population no longer care about the incident, and I'll tell you something, those Argentine citizens who do still bear resentment over that foolishness don't hold their grudge against you or the United Kingdom, but against the Argentine generals who started such a senseless war and sent so many of our brave young men needlessly to their deaths."

The actual dining portion of the state dinner had concluded, and people were mixing and mingling. A small but growing crowd of dignitaries, international guests and their entourages was gathering to listen to the two diplomats' impromptu debate. It was a subject of much recent controversy. The Briton regarded the Argentine coolly. "Indeed, I want you to know that I harbor every belief that the people of Argentina have no wish to engage in another conflict over the Falkland Islands. However, it isn't the people of Argentina who are attempting to purchase American nuclear-powered hunter-killer submarines, but their elected government."

The Argentine ambassador visibly controlled himself. "The submarines my government has expressed interest in are indeed nuclear powered, Mr. Boorthwick. However, they are not nuclear armed. It's your government, not mine, that has maintained a fleet of nuclear ballistic missile submarines long after the end of the cold war and the fall of the Soviet Union. My government has no interest in weapons of mass destruction."

The Briton's brow furrowed. The assassin smiled inwardly. The point had been deftly scored. The British Foreign Secretary had been a longtime and outspoken proponent of nuclear disarmament. Being reminded of his own country's nuclear deterrence obviously galled him. Señor Obradors's point about the nature of the submarines was true, but something of a non sequitur. It was merely a clever deflection from the point at hand. The submarines the Argentine government was expressing interest in were indeed hunter-killers. Their tactical role was to silently hunt surface ships and other submarines and destroy them either with torpedoes or antiship missiles. The British maintained a fleet of such hunter-killer submarines themselves, but they also maintained a fleet of ballistic missile submarines, each armed with sixteen Trident long-range ballistic missiles, in turn armed with multiple thermonuclear warheads.

For the United Kingdom, the thought of Argentina acquiring nuclear-powered hunter-killer submarines was sobering indeed. Had the Argentine navy had such weapons at their disposal during the Falkland Islands War, the conflict might have been very different. If they attempted such an invasion again, these new weapons could go out and engage a returning British fleet long before it ever reached the disputed islands. They could also engage England's own hunter-killer submarines, which still patrolled the South Atlantic. Nuclear attack submarines had been England's ace card during the war and had forced the Argentine navy to keep its distance. Argentina's own fleet would be a tremendous equalizer in any second conflict. The assassin suppressed another smile. The killer didn't believe that Argentine people had any wish to try to retake the Falkland Islands. Everything Señor Obradors had said was true, and unlike Mr. Boorthwick, the assassin didn't believe for a second that the democratically elected government of Argentina had any wish to invade the Falklands either.

Not yet, anyway.

Mr. Boorthwick frowned. "Then of what possible use could these submarines be to your nation?"

Señor Obradors was ready for that question. "My nation has over three thousand kilometers of coastline. We still have border disputes with Chile both in the Andes mountains in the west and in the islands of Tierra del Fuego in the south. It's my belief that even as Argentina becomes more of a world power, South America as a continent grows less and less stable. Argentina is a large nation with a small population. We have vast natural resources. We, alone, have the capacity to feed much of the world, and we do. Many of our resources have yet to be developed; many more have yet to be discovered. What kind of aggression such wealth in land and resources will attract in the upcoming millennium I can't predict but no doubt, it will attract it."

The ambassador took a deep breath and modified his tone. "We're a shipping nation. The security of our ports, our coastline and our commercial lanes are key to our development. The few diesel-electric submarines in our fleet are aging, as are the majority of our ships. Our navy must maintain a viable deterrent capability against foreign aggression in the years to come. We intend to do so, Mr. Boorthwick, and we don't intend our deterrence to be based upon the primitive and outdated philosophies of the cold war and backed up with weapons of mass destruction.''

Boorthwick's frown turned to a genuine scowl as the nuclear weapons issue was rubbed in his face again.

The assassin was pleased with the exchange. If indeed that was the sentiment in Argentina, it was going to make what was to come much easier.

Señor Obradors seemed pleased as well, and decided to end the debate while he held the upper hand. ''Good evening, Mr. Boorthwick.''

The Argentine ambassador turned on his heel and strode away. The assassin broke from the small crowd and followed him at a discreet distance. When the ambassador moved toward a hostess with a tray of champagne glasses, the assassin spoke quietly in Spanish. ''Ambassador Obradors?''

The Argentine turned and smiled happily at the assassin. ''Yes?''

''You have a phone call. I believe it's from Buenos Aires, from the office of the president.''

''Ah,'' Obradors sighed as he straightened. ''Is there someplace where I can take this privately?''

The assassin bowed slightly. ''Please allow me, Ambassador. I'll show you.''

''Thanks.''

The assassin led the ambassador to the killing ground. The room was a small, well-appointed study off the main hall. It was walled with bookshelves and sparsely furnished with little save a small antique table and two overstuffed chairs. More importantly, it had a window. One that opened into an alley that led to the easily scalable wall that surrounded the grounds. It was an excellent escape route, but only in an emergency. The assassin intended to stay and enjoy the party.

The killer gestured to the phone on the table. Dedicated electronics experts had worked diligently to break into the building's phone system and usurp the line in the study. A small red light flashed on the phone's face. The assassin smiled warmly. "Line two, Ambassador."

The Argentine smiled back as he passed into the room. "Many thanks." As the ambassador turned his back the assassin slapped a palm across his mouth and yanked his head back. Obradors let out a muffled sound of surprise as the assassin drove a knee brutally into his kidney. Obradors went rigid in agony. The commando knife whispered out of its concealed sheath and into the killer's hand. The ambassador sagged as the blade sank into his back all the way to the hilt. The assassin deliberately had slid the knife in at a bad angle and the double-edged blade grated the ambassador's spinal vertebrae. With the blade jammed solidly between two vertebrae, the assassin yanked. The thin blade snapped, leaving the first two inches of the blade embedded between the bones.

The ambassador weakly flailed his arms. The assassin yanked Obradors's head back and pulled the broken remnant of the commando knife across the Argentine's throat. Obradors went limp as his carotid opened beneath the razor sharp shard of steel. The assassin let the ambassador down gently onto the Persian carpet face first. The assassin had skillfully remained unstained by blood but made no effort to prevent the dead ambassador from bleeding in all directions once he was on the floor.

The more shocking the scene looked, the better.

The assassin peeked out the door. The hall was off the main reception area and deserted. The killer walked casually down the hallway and stopped in a bathroom for a quick check to see if there were any telltale bloodstains. Satisfied, he then followed the hall around the building, pausing a moment in an alcove as some guests left the dining room and came down the hall. A diplomat was pointing out some of the paintings on the walls. The killer remained unseen.

When they passed, the assassin stepped out of the shadows and rejoined the party. Five minutes later, the killer's head raised with everyone else's as the screaming began.

**1**

*Buenos Aires, Argentina*

Mack Bolan's gaze swept across the room. The ballroom was filled with men in tuxedos and women in black dresses. There were representatives from every nation in South America and much of Europe, as well. Throughout the hall, diamonds glittered in competition with the chandeliers and champagne flutes. The muted sound of the tango came from the string assembly that played on the raised dais, and the smoke of Cuban cigars filled the air. Bolan smiled. In South America, the rich tended to be very rich, just as the poor tended to be very poor. South Americans also knew how to throw a great party. The event was stocked with three things in abundance: liquor, beautiful women and the talk of war. His smile thinned as he scanned the room again.

Mack Bolan was looking for an assassin.

David McCarter strolled up with an enormous brandy snifter in his hand. Bolan admired his style. The leader of Stony Man Farm's Phoenix Force wore a tuxedo with the same studied ease he wore eighty pounds of weapons and gear in tropical fire zones. The former-SAS operative considered formal dinners and jungle warfare equally dangerous activities. Being a British citizen in the current company had turned the party into a social minefield for McCarter. The Briton scanned the room and grinned. "Nice party."

Bolan nodded as he saw what McCarter was grinning at.

Argentina had a well-deserved reputation for stunningly beautiful women. Some of the sleekest women Bolan had ever seen prowled the party and hung on the arms of the well-to-do in every direction. "You see any likely suspects?"

McCarter continued to survey the room. His eyes kept stopping on women. "Well, I had a number of prospects until I opened my mouth and they heard my accent," McCarter said, grinning. "Except for those two over there. They're being very diplomatic about the whole thing."

McCarter raised his glass. Across the room a devastatingly beautiful pair of identical twins giggled and raised their champagne flutes back. Bolan rolled his eyes. "What's the current sentiment with the rest of the locals?"

"Well, I keep assuring everyone I talk to that England is a nation that wishes for peace and that we have no intention of trying to deny Argentina her place as a world power, much less start a second conflict with them."

"And?"

"They smile at me tolerantly."

Bolan sighed. He had to admit it looked pretty bad. The Argentine ambassador had been assassinated in textbook SAS-commando style. Even worse, the assassin had left part of his weapon in the ambassador's spine, and it had been positively identified as a British Fairbairn-Sykes commando dagger. This was all the proof that the Argentine people had needed. Nationalism had swept like a wildfire through the provinces, and the capital city of Buenos Aires was besieged by daily anti-UK demonstrations. The Argentine government was trying to be more circumspect, but they were appalled and clearly suspicious.

Someone was trying to start a war.

McCarter looked at his empty glass. "I'm going to try to instill more goodwill. I'll let you know if I see or hear anything interesting."

"Good luck."

McCarter wandered back into the crowd. Bolan looked at his lukewarm champagne and decided it needed refreshing. As he turned, an incredibly beautiful woman stood before him challengingly. She spoke in clear but accented English. "Why does your government wish to start a war with my country?"

Bolan smiled. "My government considers both Argentina and the United Kingdom valued friends and trading partners. We're willing to do almost anything to achieve a diplomatic solution to the current crisis between your two nations."

The woman's incredibly dark eyes blinked. "Oh! You're American!" A blush rose from her collarbone and tinted her olive complexion. "You'll have to forgive me. The champagne has made me very bold."

"You speak excellent English."

"Thank you. You speak like a diplomat, but you don't look like one."

"Just what do I look like?"

The woman pointed across the room at McCarter's back. "Like him. Except that you are an American."

Bolan extended a hand. "My name is Belasko. Mike Belasko. I'm with the State Department."

The woman took Bolan's hand and pulled him forward to kiss him on the cheek. "My name is Cecilia Perez. I am a model, but I would like to go to America and become an actress. But my agent says my accent is too thick, and everyone in California is blond." Her blush deepened. "I dyed my hair blond once. I looked ridiculous."

"Not everyone in California is blond."

The woman smiled and looked out at the dance floor. Only a few pairs were moving slowly to the music. "Do you tango?"

"I'm afraid I don't."

The woman raised an eyebrow. "That's unfortunate. However, I'm prepared to forgive you. This party is much too stuffy. Would you like to go out on the veranda?"

"Very much."

Bolan followed her across the floor toward a pair of glass doors. "What is it you do for the State Department?"

"Well, normally I push a lot of paper around. Frankly, I don't know how I got invited to this party. I think I'm just supposed to smile a lot and say the United States loves everybody."

Bolan opened the door for her and they stepped out onto the veranda. Wide marble stairs led down to a well-manicured lawn and garden. A cold breeze blew across the veranda and the woman shivered.

"Are you cold?"

"No." She shook her head and smiled. "It's invigorating. Tell me, what do people in the United States think of the current situation?"

"Most Americans like England as a general rule, and though I'm ashamed to say it, most of us know little or nothing about your country."

Perez sighed. "Oh, well. Most Argentines only know of the United States from television. I suspect there is much more to your country than what one sees on *Baywatch*."

"Well, I'd like to think there is a little more to us than that." Bolan decided to do some polling of his own. "Tell me, how do you really feel about this situation?"

"Well, to be—"

Bolan whirled. The slight shadowing of the light coming through the window was enough to trigger the Executioner's combat instincts. The scrape of a shoe on the marble was enough to confirm it. A dress shoe would click on the marble. Ambushes on nearly every continent in the world had taught Bolan that a scraping footfall was a failed attempt at stealth.

The soldier slanted his body away from the attack.

A club thrust past his throat, missing by inches. On the tip of the black rubber club were a pair of stubby metal prongs.

Blue light pulsed between them and the snapping of electricity sounded like an angry hornet.

Bolan seized the man's wrist and slapped his palm up underneath the ambusher's elbow. The joint hyperextended ninety degrees and shattered. The Executioner yanked the injured arm as he whirled and knelt. The man sailed over Bolan's shoulder and landed on the marble veranda with bone-shattering force. The Executioner was already rising as the second man closed.

Playtime was over. The second attacker swung his stun gun like a truncheon at Bolan's skull. The Executioner took the blow on his forearm and shot his other hand into the man's throat. The ambusher gagged as his trachea compressed inward. The soldier sank his fingers into the man's throat and lifted. As the man went up on his toes, Bolan kicked his legs out from under him and drove him down into the veranda next to his accomplice. The man's head bounced on the marble with awful force.

Bolan turned on the third man. The attacker had his arm beneath Perez's throat and was lifting her chin. Her lip was bleeding, and her face was very pale. The attacker's other hand held a knife to her throat. He growled in thick English. "I'll kill her."

Bolan's 9 mm Beretta 93-R appeared in his hand like a magic trick. The Executioner stepped forward without hesitation. The muzzle of the sound-suppressed pistol pointed accusingly at the attacker's forehead.

The man's voice rose slightly. "I said I'll kill her!"

Bolan kept coming. The gun never wavered. The man's hand shook, and he lost his English. "*La mato! La mato!*"

Bolan raised the muzzle of the pistol six inches away from the point between the man's eyebrows. His finger began squeezing the trigger. The man's eyes widened in horror. He shoved the woman before him as a shield and then broke for the veranda stairs. Bolan released the trigger. He took three running strides and launched himself into the air.

Bolan disliked high kicks. However, his opponent was in full flight with his back turned, and Bolan couldn't afford to let him escape into the darkness of the grounds. Nor did Bolan want to fire his pistol. His cover would be instantly compromised and there would be many questions from the authorities.

Jack Grimaldi was one of the best kickers Bolan had ever encountered, and he had taken many a beating in sparring practice from the Stony Man pilot. Grimaldi had taught Bolan his theory about high kicks. Never kick up at someone. It exposed the family jewels to imminent catastrophe. Jack Grimaldi's wisdom on high kicks was simple. If he had to kick high, never kick up; instead, jump high and kick down.

Bolan pulled his right knee into his chest as he flew over the stairs. His prey was four steps lower and was stupid enough to snap a look over his shoulder at the pursuit. Bolan hurtled in and thrust his foot between the man's shoulder blades with all of his two-hundred-plus pounds behind it.

The man's arms flailed, and his chest heaved forward under the force of the blow. His legs splayed out from under him and he fell face first into the steps and rolled down them in a tangle of limbs. Bolan himself nearly went for a ride down the marble staircase as he tried to check his momentum and land on the uneven terrain. He windmilled his arms and sat on his heels in a bone-jarring crouch.

The Executioner rose with his pistol in his hand. The man lay unmoving at the bottom of the stairs. The other attackers lay at the top of the landing. One was motionless. The other moaned weakly and twitched. The soldier looked up at the woman. She held a hand to her bleeding lip and stared at him in open-mouthed shock. Bolan considered his options. He didn't have time for an interrogation, nor did he think he could manage to locate McCarter and cart off one or all of the attackers with the woman looking on.

Bolan holstered his pistol and unclipped both from his belt and put them in his jacket pocket. He went back up to the veranda. "Are you all right?"

The woman nodded unsteadily. "I think so."

"Good, let's go back inside."

Bolan draped his coat across her shaking shoulders and led her back to the party. The music had stopped and the entire crowd was facing the bandstand. A red-faced man was speaking, and the crowd was silent as they followed his every word. A man in a tuxedo turned as he felt the draft from the open door. He stared at the expression on the woman's face and the blood on her lip. She was going into shock. Bolan spoke with the tone of command. "This woman has been attacked. Call the police." The man swallowed and gestured at one of the hostesses.

Several others had turned to see what was going on, and murmurs of indignation spread. However, nearly all eyes stayed on the bandstand. Bolan had learned Spanish the hard way in places like Colombia and Mexico. The speaker was orating in such impassioned, rapid-fire Castilian that Bolan could hardly follow it. McCarter's voice spoke low from behind him as a small crowd gathered around the girl. "Are you all right?"

Bolan's hand went into his pocket and he discreetly put the pistol and its holster into McCarter's hand. The Phoenix Force leader made them disappear without a word. Bolan edged closer. "We were attacked on the veranda. Three men. All down."

"You? The girl? Or you and the girl."

Bolan was willing to bet a great deal that ambush had been for him.

He spoke quietly to McCarter. "What's happened here?"

The woman winced as someone poured some brandy down

her and it stung her bloody lip. The speaker on the dais waved his hands dramatically. People in the audience began waving their fists.

McCarter's face was serious as a tombstone. "It's bad."

"What is it?"

"The Argentine ambassador to the United States has been assassinated."

**2**

*São Paulo, Brazil*

"The man is no goddamned attaché of the American State Department!"

Waldemar Salome nodded patiently. He was a tall, lean man with long black hair and eyes as flat and black as a shark's. He sat at an immense table in his house in the mountains above the city. Other members of the cabal he led sat around the table, all of them wore disturbed looks on their faces.

The man's voice rose. "He destroyed the imbeciles you sent me! He tore them limb from limb! With his bare hands!"

The rest of the men of the war council kept their eyes down and their thoughts to themselves as the man ranted. The way he was yelling in Salome's face was brave to the point of recklessness. Ladislao Dirazar was an intense man. He was Argentine and ran much of the cabal's operations in Buenos Aires. They all wondered how many more seconds Dirazar was going to live.

Behind Salome stood four of his bodyguards. The *Indios*. Their flat faces and Mongol-like eyes showed nothing. What was said in council didn't concern them. They spoke no Spanish, and even their Portuguese was limited to a primitive pidgin language used in trading. They spoke their own tribal dialect born in the basin of the Amazon rain forest. It was a dialect Salome had taken great pains to learn. He had taken these men from the squalor of their reservations and given them guns to kill their enemies and money for their families. He had taken his chosen soldiers out of the rain forest and given them women with golden hair, fancy clothes and riches beyond their comprehension. To these stone-faced warriors, Waldemar Salome was the river of life for themselves and their families back home. He was a god walking the earth, and he was a god of war. Their only loyalty was to him, their only responsibility was to kill anyone Salome wished. They were incorruptible bodyguards and stone-faced executioners. They feared nothing.

Behind their inscrutable expressions, they were very aware that the city boy was showing a lack of respect for their patron. The *Indios* stood with their arms folded, and their fingers crept under their Armani jackets to the grips of their 9 mm pistols. They patiently awaited the signal to kill Dirazar.

Salome steepled his fingers. "Yes, I'm aware of what happened."

Dirazar waved his hands. "Limb from limb! Like rag dolls!"

"Indeed." Salome indeed knew of this. His best man, Rafa, had gone to the hospital in Buenos Aires and confirmed it. Put together, the medical reports were an amazing amalgamation of broken bones, cracked ribs, dislocated joints and fractured skulls. Salome, himself, knew a great deal about killing with hands and feet. This was very impressive. The men he had sent had been Paraguayans. The Paraguayans were a poor people. Many of them immigrated to Argentina, and in particular to Buenos Aires, where they took jobs that most Argentines were too proud to soil themselves with. It had been easy to smuggle them onto the grounds as servants. The Paraguayans weren't experienced street soldiers, but in the past they had shown great talent at kidnapping and torture. Their talent had seemed to run out at a very inopportune time, and sadly, in the next two hours, all three of them would conveniently succumb to their injuries and die before they had a chance to be interviewed by the police.

Salome decided not to have Dirazar killed for his impertinence. "I agree with you, Ladislao. The man's performance at the party proves he is no employee of the American State Department. It leads me to wonder what an American of such obvious skill was doing there."

It was a question that bothered everyone at the table. The cabal had counted on the United States doing nothing as the plan unfolded and then exploded in the world's face. Now it appeared the Americans had somehow entered the game. Salome almost smiled. Though outwardly the mission was a wash, they had uncovered something which appeared to be much more interesting than the intended victim.

"You say he was seen speaking with the Briton?"

Dirazar managed to calm himself. "Yes, and I'm willing to bet that the Briton is some kind of operative as well."

"I trust you have both the American and the British Embassies in Buenos Aires under observation."

Dirazar looked vaguely offended. "Of course."

"Good." Salome came to a decision. They had rattled a cage and a tiger had come out. Perhaps it was time to tear open the cage and see what else spilled out. "I believe I wish to focus on this Briton for the moment rather than risk alerting the Americans any further."

Dirazar perked an eyebrow. "You have something in mind?"

"Indeed, the Argentine people are very upset, and rightly so. Two of their ambassadors have been heinously assassinated by the cowardly British. The politicians do nothing except argue among themselves and whine about diplomatic channels and the United Nations. The people are ready. They're already protesting daily in the streets outside the capitol building and the British Embassy." Salome smiled. "I believe it's about time we had a riot."

*Buenos Aires, Argentina*

"THEY WANTED YOU ALIVE."

Mack Bolan sat back and sipped a Quilmes beer in the secure communications room of the U.S. Embassy. The satellite link with Stony Man Farm was clear despite being a quarter of a planet away. Aaron Kurtzman pondered the situation from his end in Virginia. "Two of them had stun guns. The knife only came out after you had downed the first two."

"Or they wanted her alive. Or both of us."

McCarter scratched his mustache. "Why would they want her?"

Bolan shrugged. "It's hard to imagine why anyone would be dumb or desperate enough to try to kidnap a would-be actress at a state dinner. Or me for that matter. I can't imagine anyone at the party knowing who I really am or what McCarter and I represent. Even if an enemy from a past operation was there for some reason, it would be an awfully big freak of fate that they just happened to have a kidnap team in place that night."

McCarter leaned back in his chair. "Maybe the girl knew something. Or has dirt on somebody. You said she's a model and wants to be an actress. That fits the mold of a professional escort. Maybe she witnessed something, or someone she's been 'escorting' whispered in her ear something he shouldn't have."

"That's possible. But why three men with stun guns big enough to stop a horse? Chloroform would be quieter. It seems to me they were expecting to take someone down hard."

"Stun guns are good for more than just incapacitation, they're good for torturing out information as well."

Bolan conceded the point.

Kurtzman pondered what the two men were saying. "So,

we have three bad guys with stun guns lurking in the bushes outside the party.''

''So it seems.''

McCarter jumped in. ''The question is, why?''

Bolan finished his beer. ''They were waiting.''

''Obviously.''

''They wouldn't be waiting out in the wind for just anybody who came strolling out on the veranda. They had to have had some way of predicting their quarry was coming,'' Kurtzman suggested.

''I don't think they were targeting me.'' Bolan smiled at McCarter. ''I think they were targeting you.''

McCarter raised an eyebrow. ''Really?''

''I went outside with a beautiful woman, and I was almost immediately attacked. You had those twins making eyes at you. I think maybe one or both of them was going to lead you outside for a rendezvous with our friends. Only I went out with the wrong girl.''

Kurtzman was intrigued. ''That might fit. McCarter was one of the few Britons at the affair. They could well have been targeting him or one of the other British dignitaries who were present.''

McCarter took a sip of his own beer. ''It's possible, but why didn't they break off the attack when it wasn't me?''

''Maybe they didn't know, or maybe at that point they didn't care. Maybe they just wanted to silence me when they made their mistake.'' Bolan shrugged modestly. ''Or maybe I suddenly became more interesting.''

McCarter looked vaguely offended.

Aaron Kurtzman echoed Bolan's sentiment. ''A target of opportunity, then. That's possible. Did they have radios on them? Or any other kind of communication devices?''

''No, none that I saw. But I didn't have much time to pat them down.''

Kurtzman paused before adding, "I have some other news."

"What's that?"

"Your three dancing partners got out of the hospital."

Bolan nodded. He had expected they would check out of the hospital early and try to disappear. "Did the CIA manage to get some tails on them?"

Kurtzman's sigh was clear over the satellite. "Our boys got loaded in the meat wagon and went straight to the morgue."

Bolan should have expected that. "All three?"

"All three. Our intelligence managed to get a look at the doctor's reports. They all apparently died of complications. The one with the fractured skull died of brain hemorrhaging in the night. That I'm willing to buy, but the other two are listed as having violent allergic reactions to the painkillers they were given and died of anaphylactic shock."

"They were poisoned."

"Well, the United States doesn't exactly have a very big intelligence infrastructure down there in Argentina, so I can't confirm it immediately. As a matter of fact we probably won't ever be able to, short of clandestinely digging up the bodies and doing a covert autopsy. But at the moment, I'm willing to bet both of your paychecks on it."

Bolan nodded to himself. That didn't leave them with a whole lot of leads. The question was, what to do next? Bolan tapped a finger on the arm of his chair. "Let's go over it again."

Kurtzman sounded off what the three of them already knew. "We've got two dead Argentine ambassadors. Both assassinated commando-style. Circumstantial evidence points to British involvement."

McCarter frowned but said nothing. Kurtzman continued. "Argentina has been lobbying to buy surplus American 637 Sturgeon-class nuclear submarines. The Argentine ambassador to the United States who died last night was personally involved in lobbying the United States government to sanction the deal. By the way, the international reaction on this is starting to turn ugly. At first most of the world, and South America in particular, were opposed to the sale of the submarines. Now that Argentine diplomats are being killed many people are willing to believe that England, and perhaps other European powers, is trying to hold back South America from emerging as a major player in world politics.''

The Briton scowled. "Someone is trying to start a war.''

Bolan grimaced at the unpleasant thought.

McCarter didn't like the look on Bolan's face. "What are you thinking?''

"I'm thinking about oil.''

All three men were silent for a moment. In 1995 the United Kingdom and Argentina had decided to set up an umbrella agreement that would handle oil issues in the newly promising area of ocean southwest of the Falkland Islands, and to do so without affecting either nation's claim of sovereignty. However, another area in the South Atlantic had recently started to show even greater promise of oil wealth. It was an area of ocean just north of the Falkland Islands, and Britain considered it strictly part of its sovereign territory. In 1996 the government of the Falkland Islands had issued seven tranches to five oil groups, and none of the groups were Argentine. There was a lot of bad blood over it.

McCarter looked at Bolan long and hard. "You're thinking that the British government could actually be behind this.''

Bolan met his friend's gaze. "If the oil projections for the area are correct, we may be talking about at least one hundred thousand barrels a day. At sixteen dollars a barrel we're looking at nearly six hundred million dollars a year. You don't think there are people willing to kill for that kind of money in your country?''

McCarter smiled thinly. "It's just as likely that the Argentines are doing this themselves to set up the situation."

"Granted. I'm not accusing the British government, but we have to look at the unpleasant possibility that there may be unscrupulous individuals within the U.K. who are capable of doing what we are encountering. Under President Menem, Argentina wrote into its constitution that it would advance its claim to the Falkland Islands only by peaceful means. My hunch is that this war is being brewed for them."

Kurtzman's voice came through the receiver with what the three men had been thinking all along. "A third party."

Bolan nodded. "That's my bet."

"Who would want to start a second war between England and Argentina, and what would they hope to gain?"

Bolan rose from his chair. "That's a good question."

**3**

*Buenos Aires, Argentina*

A brick smashed into the wall of the British Embassy.

McCarter arched an eyebrow at Bolan. "This could be trouble."

That was something of an understatement. The embassy was surrounded by a horde of angry citizens. In past days they had carried banners and signs and shouted slogans of national unity while they waved the Argentine flag. College students had staged sit-ins and chained themselves to the wrought-iron fence in front of the embassy in protest. Bolan felt his stomach tighten. Today wasn't a demonstration. This was an angry mob. Bricks and bottles flew, while fists waved in the air. Political slogging was finished. The bullhorns called out for blood and vengeance. The British flag burned from a dozen poles. The crowd was working itself into a frenzy. Argentine police officers stood in a line before the embassy with helmets, clear plastic riot shields and clubs. Armored vehicles with water cannons were parked before the embassy gates. Soldiers with revolving gas grenade launchers scanned the crowd.

McCarter slowed the car. "It's been bad before, but not like this."

"They've had another ambassador killed. As far as the people are concerned their worst suspicions have been confirmed. They want blood."

"Probably mine."

"Pull over. I don't think we want to try to drive through that. Even with the soldiers there."

McCarter pulled the Citroën over to the curb near a café. "Listen Striker, perhaps we should—"

Porcelain shattered on the Citroën's windshield and coffee smeared across the glass in a brown wave. People were rising from their seats, faces twisted in anger and shouts grew louder.

"I think they've spotted our diplomatic plates."

"I think you're right."

"We should get the hell out of here, fast."

"I'm on it." Gears ground as McCarter shoved the Citroën into reverse. The car lurched backward a foot and then rocked to a halt as the Briton slammed the brake. "Damn it!"

Bolan craned his head around. A woman with a baby in her arms was behind them screaming at the top of her lungs. She began kicking the rear bumper. Café patrons had left their seats and were approaching the car. "Get us out of here, David."

"Right, I—damn it!" A pair of youths were in front of the car slamming their hands on the hood.

McCarter's face was tight as he yanked the gear stick back. "Run them down?"

Bolan snarled to himself. The last thing he wanted to do was kill Argentine civilians. He had even less fondness for the idea of being torn limb from limb by an angry mob. "Out your door! Now!"

McCarter flung open his door and leaped out. Bolan twisted in his seat and dived after him into the street. The citizens on the streets yelled as they came out of the car. Bolan rose and waved his hands in the air frantically. He dodged a plastic chair that was hurled over the car at him and his voice boomed out at parade-ground decibels.

"*Suecos! Suecos! Nosotros ser Suecos!*"

The looks of hate froze. The two youths at the front of the car blinked in confusion. A man about to throw a beer bottle stopped at half cock and peered at Bolan curiously.

Bolan waved his arms again. *"Suecos!"*

McCarter spoke out of the corner of his mouth. "What did you tell them?"

Bolan kept his hands raised and kept smiling as he whispered, "I told them we were Swedish."

"What?"

"Everybody loves Swedes."

People in the crowd looked at their feet sheepishly. Apologies began murmuring among the people gathered on the sidewalk. The crowd visibly relaxed. Bolan went to full alert as a man stepped off the sidewalk and came around the car. His lips twisted in a sneer as he pointed at McCarter and Bolan. *"Es un truco! Son Ingleses!"*

Embarrassment was replaced by confusion and renewed stares of hostility in the crowd.

McCarter looked around as the tension in the air thickened. "What did he say?"

Bolan kept the smile on his face as he shook his head and held out his hands placatingly. "He says it's a trick. He says we're English."

"So how do we play it?"

"Run!" Bolan's fingers stiffened into a blunt spear as he rammed their tips into the man's solar plexus. The man went down to his hands and knees with a strangled wheeze. Bolan and McCarter bolted into the street. Cars screeched to a halt. Horns blared as they dodged the braking vehicles. The sidewalk behind them broke into pandemonium. Curses and shouts followed as they ran. The crowd that had been watching the exchange from across the street began to move out into the first lane of traffic to cut them off.

The situation was out of control. Bolan decided not to fight it. The 9 mm Beretta 93-R machine pistol came out of his shoulder holster with the sound of ripping Velcro. The selector switch flicked to full-auto under his thumb as he ran. Bolan pulled the trigger twice and two 3-round bursts tore upward into the air sounding like ripping canvas. Civilians began screaming and running in all directions. Bolan lowered the pistol and aimed it over the heads of the milling crowd ahead of him across the street. They scattered as he touched off another 3-round burst.

In front of the embassy the mass of people surged against one another at the sound of gunfire. The riot police waded into the protesters with their clubs swinging. Water cannons blasted into the crowd and grenade launchers thumped. Cylinders of tear gas arced over the crowd trailing streamers of white gas.

"Striker!"

Bolan whirled. McCarter had gone down to one knee in the middle of the street and was already rising again. His left arm hung at his side. His 9 mm Browning Hi-Power pistol filled his other hand.

The blow took Bolan squarely in the forehead. His vision went black and he saw pinpoint purple flashes as his knees buckled beneath him. Hard-won battle instincts took over. The Beretta came up in both of his hands as he scanned his front sight across the windows above the street. People on the balconies who had been watching screamed and hurled themselves to their stomachs. Two stories above, Bolan caught the flash of sunlight on glass. The Executioner aimed low and touched off a triburst. A figure staggered out of the darkened room and onto the balcony. The man in a dark suit clutched a compact rifle with a telescopic sight. The rifle's barrel bulged with the thick sound suppressor built onto it.

Bolan flicked the Beretta's selector switch to semiautomatic fire and squeezed off three quickly aimed shots.

The man jerked as the 9 mm hollowpoint bullets struck him. He kept staggering forward and went headfirst over the balcony. Patrons who had stayed on the patio of the café screamed as the man crashed into one of the tables.

"McCarter! Let's move!"

The Briton broke into a run. The mob was fleeing the police and hundreds of people suddenly swarmed around them as they fled the tear gas and the water cannons. Bolan and McCarter joined the swarm and let the flow of the herd take them down the street. Traffic was stalled in both lanes as screaming people ran among the cars in all directions. Bolan used his strength to shove his way to the Phoenix Force leader. He holstered his pistol and kept ahold of the Briton's good arm. He shouted in McCarter's ear above the sound of the riot.

"Are you all right?"

"Took one through the arm!"

Bolan yanked him up onto the sidewalk and through the door of a coffee shop, where people lined the windows of the café watching the screaming, running mob. They stared at both soldiers. Bolan ignored them and moved straight through the shop and down a narrow hallway. The hall lead to a back door. Bolan put his foot to it, and it flew back on its hinges. He slammed it behind him and took a look at McCarter's arm. There was an entry wound but no exit wound on either side of the soldier's biceps.

"Can you move it?"

McCarter grimaced and flexed his arm. "Rather not."

"You'll live."

McCarter's eyes narrowed. "You all right? Your head's bleeding."

Bolan took off his cap. A trickle of blood rolled down his forehead. The swollen flesh under his fingers told him the bruising had already started. Bolan looked at his baseball cap. The gray smear of a deformed .22 caliber lead bullet had torn through the outer fabric and stopped on the Kevlar insert. The armored vest he wore beneath his jacket had stopped the bullet that impacted against his chest. "You hit anywhere else?"

"Bastard shot me four bloody times. I put up my arm when I went for my gun. I think he had figured out I was wearing armor and went for the headshot."

Bolan looked at his hat. The assassin's second shot had torn a long furrow in the fabric along the top. The killer had certainly not messed around. He had made two very real attempts to blow Bolan's head off. "They were waiting for us."

McCarter raised his head as sirens began to wail in the distance. "They've been watching your embassy. When we came out of the car they radioed their friend with the rifle."

"They were betting on us stopping the car when we saw the mob. If the sniper didn't get a clear shot at us when things got hot, the tattletale was going to follow us through the crowd and give it to us in the back of the head. I'm betting they had the back entrance covered as well."

"Well, they took a bloody good stab at it, I'll give them that. I don't much like the idea of going back and giving them a second shot at us."

"Neither do I. I say we find a phone. We'll see if Stony Man Farm can set up a safehouse for us. Think you can keep from bleeding to death until then?"

"I'll have a lash at it."

Bolan bound McCarter's arm with a handkerchief and gave him his jacket. He folded McCarter's bloodstained coat and pushed it into a trash Dumpster. "Let's get out of here."

"What's the plan?"

"Lay low, get you cleaned up." Bolan looked up and down the alley. "Then we'll see what develops."

**4**

*São Paulo, Brazil*

The men around the table feared for their lives. Waldemar Salome wasn't pleased. It would have been better if he was jumping up and down, screaming obscenities and foaming at the mouth. Instead he sat in silence. His eyes burned a hole in the wall, staring into some terrible distance where life and death was decided. He radiated cold fury. Four of the *Indio* bodyguards stood behind him. Two more by the door. They stood like stone Buddhas. Their expressionless, almond-shaped eyes were as implacable as death. They knew the mood of the great man and they awaited his signal. The men around the table tried not to look at them. None of them could meet Salome's eyes. Twice, Salome had given them orders. Twice, they had failed.

Someone was going to be killed.

Ladislao Dirazar was fairly certain it would be him. His confederates around the table were once again impressed by his bravery. It was amazing he had shown up for this meeting at all. Most of them had thought he would disappear into the vast Argentine interior of Patagonia and pray that Salome never found him. A trickle of sweat ran down Dirazar's temple despite the air-conditioning. Other than that, he seemed remarkably composed.

"Why is the Briton not in our hands or dead?" The men around the table jumped as Salome spoke. His voice was eerily conversational. He might well have been asking about the weather.

Dirazar steeled himself and met his master's gaze. "The Briton is a special forces operative. So is the American."

"I have considered that possibility. But that doesn't answer my question."

Dirazar wiped his brow with the back of his hand. "I believe it does. The Paraguayans were kidnappers. The men we sent into Buenos Aires were political assassins. Both groups have served us well in the past, however, our targets weren't plantation owners or businessmen whose families needed kidnapping. Nor were they some local politician or judge who wasn't playing ball with us. Our mistake was sending thugs and assassins against special forces soldiers. The special forces of England and the United States are the best in the world. We all know this. They aren't only the most effective combat soldiers in the world, they are also highly trained in activities such as escape and evasion. Our men were simply outclassed."

"They had surprise."

Dirazar swallowed. He wasn't a trained soldier. He was a career criminal, and had risen high enough to be brought into Salome's fold. However, he had killed, and over the years his competitors had tried to kill him as well. He knew from hard experience that surprise was the greatest weapon in the world. In Buenos Aires, against these new opponents, it hadn't been enough. He cleared his throat. "Our sniper got off six shots. Our observers saw the Briton go down. They swear the American was hit as well. Our sniper was three stories up and across the boulevard. The American took him out with a handgun."

"A lucky shot." Gordo spoke. He had helped Dirazar orchestrate the assassination attempt. He had considered the plan excellent and was very angry that it had failed. His anger was mixed with the fear that the *Indios* would drag him outside and shoot him on the lawn like a dog.

Dirazar sighed. "Three lucky shots."

Gordo tried to salvage himself. "They must have been wearing armor. As you say, our observers saw them take hits."

Salome steepled his fingers and peered at Dirazar. The Argentine fought the urge to squirm and look away from the flat, sharklike gaze of Salome's eyes. His master spoke. "I'm open to suggestions."

The tension around the table fell away as if it had been cut by a knife. The meeting was no longer a death sentence trial. It was a council of war again. Dirazar had to fight another urge to collapse in his chair and pant with nervous exhaustion. His mind sought a suggestion that would help ensure his continued existence. Gordo beat him to it. "We have men watching both the British and American Embassies. The agents must be laying low now, but they will eventually return to one or the other. Coming or going we can make another attempt."

Dirazar shook his head. "They'll be waiting for that. In fact they'll count on it. Barring some sort of extraordinary event they still have no leads about who we are and what we represent. I don't think we should give them any."

Gordo's chair squealed in protest as he shifted his massive bulk back into it. "I see what you are saying, Ladislao, but I don't believe we can have foreign special forces operatives poking about in the dark, either. We have spent millions on this endeavor. I believe we have been very careful, but, as everyone here knows, no plan is perfect, and it is possible, indeed probable, that both men will have the entire intelligence resources of the United States and the United Kingdom at their disposal. I suggest we remove them from the situation before they become a real threat."

Dirazar shook his head. "Risky. It could create more problems than it would solve."

The fat man mopped his brow with a handkerchief. "I believe an antitank rocket could solve all of the problems. For that matter, a truck bomb blowing up one or both of the embassies would solve our problem, as well as add fuel to the international situation."

Dirazar regarded Gordo warily. His reputation for ruthlessness was well earned.

Salome looked at the two men. Dirazar didn't like killing when a deal could be made instead. Gordo enjoyed killing. His sadistic streak was as wide as his waistband. Their differing viewpoints made for good council. Between the two of them Salome usually found the third choice. "I have a better idea."

Everyone at the table sat up very straight. "What our opponents want more than anything is a lead. We'll give them one. Then kill them at a time and place of our own choosing."

*Buenos Aires, Argentina*

MACK BOLAN sat cross-legged on the floor and stared at the computer screen. He vainly wished Gadgets Schwarz would magically materialize. Bolan had learned a great deal about computers since the founding of Stony Man Farm, but it was still not his area of expertise. The laptop computer before him had cables snaking out of it in all directions. Three large aluminum suitcases surrounded the laptop, containing hard drives, a fax machine, a scrambler, decoder and satellite links that increased the laptop's capabilities far beyond its small size. There were sovereign nations on the planet that had less computing power than Bolan had on the floor of the town house. The soldier adjusted a connection and pressed the enter key. The computer before him chimed and welcomed him to the Stony Man mainframe. It also opened up a real-time video link with the Farm.

Bolan leaned back as Aaron Kurtzman's face blinked at him. Kurtzman wasn't a particularly handsome man to begin with. He was less so at four o'clock in the morning, Virginia time. "Morning, Striker. Where are you?"

"We're in a CIA safehouse in San Telmo. It's a district of Buenos Aires. It's the Argentine equivalent of Haight-Ashbury. All the artists and Bohemians live here. It's the birthplace of the tango."

"Really?"

"Bear, we're starting to develop something of a situation here."

"So I've gathered. Barbara is already flying you and McCarter both a second load of gear to keep in the safehouse. I figured you might be a little leery of going back to either of the embassies."

"I am. I only want to do that if no other way of generating a lead presents itself."

Kurtzman frowned. Sticking one's head out to see who tried to blow it off was an ugly way to try to generate a lead. He had watched Bolan do it too many times to count. Sooner or later the big guy's luck had to fail. "What can I do from my end?"

"I want anything the embassy tries to tell me to get bounced to the Farm and then to the safehouse here through our scrambler."

"You think the embassies are bugged?"

"Show me one that isn't. It looks like whoever we're up against wants to start a war. They almost have to have some kind of connection with the Argentine military. It wouldn't suprise me if they've bought off someone in the British Embassy as well. I don't want a direct link to where we are unless I choose to reveal it. You're going to be our cutout."

"Done."

"I also need a list of all U.S. military and intelligence assets here in Argentina. Give me everything the British have as well."

"That's not going to be hard. As I mentioned the United States just doesn't have much of a presence down there. Almost all intelligence resources allocated to South America go to Colombia and the other nations where we're fighting the drug war. Frankly, Argentina hasn't been part of our intelligence loop in any significant way since World War II. As for military assets, we have even less. We've got a military attaché at the embassy of course, and some Marine guards. We occasionally have some training teams down there. The Argentine air force still uses A-4 Skyhawks and arms them with U.S. ordnance. Sometimes we have some of our Air Force boys down there on servicing and training missions."

Bolan filed that away for future reference. "Anything else?"

"You're at the bottom of the world, Striker. We just don't have much down there. I'll see if we have anything in the private sector that could be of use to you, but don't hold your breath. As for British assets, well, they hardly have anything down there at all except their embassy, and like you saw, it's under siege at the moment."

"I need a lead, Bear. We're in the dark on this one, and so far they've been calling all the shots. I need a leg up on the power curve or we're going to have a war on our hands."

"I've got something. It's not much, and frankly I don't like it."

"What?"

"Well, you've been incommunicado with the embassy lately, haven't you?"

"We called once to confirm we were still alive, and then we communicated with a CIA agent through pay phones. He managed to get our gear shipped out of the embassy. They took it to the airport and chartered a helicopter. They flew into the outer capital area and then took a series of cars and trains to get us our computer equipment and some heavier weapons. I told them not to contact us here except through you unless it was code red. This ate up the last few hours. I didn't want any contact until I set up the link with you.''

''Well, Striker, you've had a visitor at the U.S. Embassy.''

''Who?''

''A woman. She says her name is Cecilia Perez. She matches the description of the woman you were with when you were attacked at the party a couple of nights ago. She showed up asking for Mike Belasko.''

Bolan's eyes narrowed. ''What does she want?''

''She says she's being followed. She thinks someone is trying to kill her.''

**5**

Bolan kept his knees bent and stayed low in the crowd as he stepped onto the train platform. Buenos Aires had a very effective subway system. He stopped behind a pillar between the train and the waiting area. The soldier examined the people. Only one person was obviously armed, and that was a transit cop. Bolan shook his head. They certainly had a different way of doing things in South America. The transit officer wore a tight, knee-length black skirt below her blue uniform blouse and high heels. There would have been police union strikes all across the United States if female officers were required to look as lady-like as they appeared to be in Argentina. There was no way she could ever run down a perp in her outfit. Then again, maybe she didn't have to. She also had a Browning Hi-Power automatic strapped to her hip, and a locally made copy of the Israeli 9 mm Uzi submachine gun strapped over her shoulder next to her purse. She was lounging against a token booth, studying herself in the mirror of her compact and applying lipstick with a critical eye. She scanned the platform intently for a moment as the train debarked, and then went back to examining her lips with intense concentration.

Bolan swept his gaze over the back of the platform where there was a row of benches. Cecilia Perez was sitting and looking wildly through the crowd of people. Her eyes were wide and her head kept darting about. Her hair was disheveled and her eyes were puffy from crying.

Bolan waited as his backup fanned on both sides and put the platform in a cross fire. Marine Corps Embassy Guards Samuels and Harris were moving out and trying to look inconspicuous in plainclothes. The two Marines wore jeans, athletic shoes and vinyl jackets with Argentine soccer team logos on them. Beneath their jackets each man carried a pair of Colt .45 automatics and tear gas grenades. Bolan had a great deal of faith in United States Marines, but they weren't his first choice for undercover operatives. Their barrel chests, perfect posture and crew cuts screamed *semper fidelis* despite their casual clothes. Samuels was also black, and there were almost no people of color in Argentina. Samuels attracted attention. Much of it was admiring, but attention was something they couldn't afford.

Bolan moved to flank Perez.

The woman searched the crowd with increasing desperation as the train finished loading and the doors hissed shut. Both Samuels and Harris had been shown sketches of her. On cue, Harris walked past her and stopped to ask for a cigarette. Bolan scanned the area once again for snipers. There were no good hides for a concealed shooter. If there was going to be an ambush, it was going to be a slap-leather situation rather than a sniping. If someone was watching the girl, their eyes would be on her and Harris.

Bolan moved.

Harris walked a few feet away and then turned back. Samuels sidled up right on cue. Both Marines now formed human shields for Bolan and the girl.

Bolan spoke quietly. "Cecilia."

When she saw Bolan was almost right next to her, she leaped to her feet. "You came!" She beelined straight at him as if she were going to leap into his arms.

Bolan's right hand was in his jacket pocket. The grip of his Beretta 93-R filled his hand. He tilted his hand up and pointed the corner of his jacket ever so slightly at the girl. "*Despacio.*"

Her eyes flew wide as she halted, and then she came forward slowly as Bolan had commanded. He kept his voice low. "Get on the next train. Get off at the next exit. There is a cab waiting for you. There will be two men in it. One has red hair. Get in the cab."

Bolan broke away and walked directly to the transit officer. "Which train do I take to get to Adrogue?"

The policewoman beamed at Bolan. "You're an American?"

Bolan smiled and nodded. The officer smiled wider and began giving him directions. The Executioner kept an eye on the platform. Perez looked confused but had risen and gone to the edge of the platform. Bolan chatted up the policewoman. She took out her pad and pencil and wrote down the directions for him even though they involved only a single change of trains. The next train came by and Perez got on it. Harris boarded as well at the far end of the car. Bolan and Samuels continued to keep each other covered. The train pulled away from the platform and the policewoman pulled the sheet of paper from her pad. She smiled at Bolan happily. She had written her name and phone number on the paper.

Samuels headed for the stairs. Bolan waited thirty seconds and then followed. McCarter was waiting in a rented Renault with the engine running. Bolan slid into the car quickly as he scanned the street. "Drive."

"THEY WERE IN MY apartment! They tore apart everything. They are following me! I know it!" Perez burst into tears again. She lost her English and began speaking Castilian Spanish so fast Bolan couldn't understand it. Bolan and McCarter exchanged looks across the table. They sat in a very expensive café in the town of El Tigre. The town was an upscale resort area half an hour north of Buenos Aires on the

Rio de la Plata. They had taken a twisting route to get here, and halfway there they had fallen into a loose tail behind Perez's cab. McCarter was one of the best drivers Bolan had ever met, offensively and defensively. The Phoenix Force leader was ninety percent sure they hadn't been followed.

El Tigre had other benefits. It was far enough away from Buenos Aires that the opposition wouldn't consider it a likely place for Bolan and company to be. The café was also directly over the river. On the dock below, Samuels and Harris waited in a rented speedboat in case they needed to make a quick getaway. Several M-16 rifles with grenade launchers attached were locked and loaded beneath the motorboat's benches.

Perez's potential as a lead was drying up very quickly. They had checked her for a wire, and Bolan had swept her with a bug detector. Unless she had something that was next-generation technology in a very discreet place, she was clean of any kind of tracking, surveillance or transmitters.

Bolan smothered his frustration and arranged a sympathetic look on his face. "So, they ransacked your apartment."

"Yes! They tore everything apart! Everything is ruined!"

"Did they take anything?"

She paused. "No, that was very strange. They took none of my money, jewelry or anything."

Bolan nodded. "Did you notice anything unusual at all? I know you were frightened, but was there anything else you can think of?"

Perez chewed her bottom lip for a moment. "Well, they tore apart my stereo and the speakers I had mounted on the walls. There were some holes cut in the walls. I thought that was strange."

McCarter looked out over the Rio de la Plata and north to Uruguay. "They were looking for surveillance gear. Video cameras are often concealed in stereo speaker housings. The holes in the walls were probably probes looking for trans-mitters or wires. It wouldn't surprise me if they installed some surveillance gear of their own before they left to see if someone besides the police came investigating.''

McCarter was right. Cecilia Perez was their only lead and the enemy knew it. Checking her apartment for clues was like grasping at straws, but it was the only thing they could do. If they did find countersurveillance gear, its design and the way it was set up could possibly give them some clues about who their adversaries were. However, going to her apartment to look for those clues was almost certainly a death trap. Bolan suspected it wouldn't be snipers or street shooters they would be facing this time either. If he were the enemy, he would put surveillance gear in Perez's apartment. He would put it somewhere not too hard to find, and he would back it up with tamper switches connected to ten or twenty kilograms of high explosive.

Bolan shook his head. "We're going to need Gadgets. We need a full suite of counterelectronic warfare equipment. We need bomb-disposal gear and Gadgets to go with it as well.''

"People in hell need ice water, but they don't often get it.'' McCarter shook his head. "And until we can get more leads, I doubt whether we can get any more man power approved.''

Perez looked back and forth at the two men in confusion. "Who are you? What's happening?''

Bolan looked at her and spoke frankly. "Someone is trying to start a war. We intend to stop them.''

"You mean between my country and England.''

"Yes. We believe the conflict is being instigated by a third party. One with a vested interest in seeing the two nations come to blows.''

"But who would do such a thing? Why?''

"Those are two very good questions.''

Perez looked close to tears again. "But what has this to do with me?''

Bolan sighed. "I'm afraid you were in the wrong place at

the wrong time. When you got involved in the attack on me at the embassy, you became a pawn in the game these people are playing.''

"Are they going to kill me?"

Bolan tried to be reassuring. The young woman had been through a lot in the past two days. "I'm not sure. They may try, but we don't intend to let them do that, either. Do you have relatives you can stay with, or friends? Someplace out of the city or in the provinces would be preferable."

Tears began spilling down her cheeks again. "My mother, she has a house in Olavarria…"

"Belasko, if they ransacked her apartment, I'm betting they took a good look at her address book. They'll be waiting for that."

Perez looked close to panic. "What am I to do? Will they kill my mother?"

"I wouldn't put anything past them. You don't have any information they want, but they could try kidnapping you or your mother to force our hand."

"We'll take you to the American Embassy. Tell your mother to take the first bus out of town in any direction. I'll have money wired to her. We can make her drop off the planet for a while."

McCarter watched the café patrons. "So how do you want to play it? You want to try her apartment?"

"No." An idea began to form in Bolan's mind. "We're getting on the horn. We need backup. I want to talk to the Bear. We're going to need Rafael and Gadgets for this one. As for going to Cecilia's apartment, that's exactly what they want. They've been calling all the shots and they've been the ones on the offensive. I'm tired of walking into situations of their choosing. Her apartment is a no-win situation. We end up blown up or shot, with nothing to show for it. They think we'll take the chance because we can't think of anything better to do.''

"Do we have something better to do?"

Bolan smiled.

## 6

Hermann "Gadgets" Schwarz, Rafael Encizo and Akira Tokaido had just spent fourteen hours on an airplane. Schwarz looked distinctly grumpy. Encizo smiled as he looked around the safehouse. It had been a long time since he had been in Argentina. It was a country he had always been fond of. Schwarz sat heavily into a chair and gratefully accepted the beer McCarter handed him. "So what are we going to do?"

"For starters we're going to break into the Buenos Aires city morgue," Bolan answered. "We're going to see if we can get some IDs on the boys who have been taking shots at us."

Encizo wiped his brow in the heat. "From the file I read on the plane, you've identified the first attackers as Paraguayan nationals."

"That was the first bunch, but I want to find out what organization they belong to. I want to find out more about the boys who took a shot at us during the riot. I have a feeling they were more local. Someone had to have hired them. Then we start working our way up the ladder."

Schwarz frowned. "There's got to be cutouts along the way if these guys have any brains at all, and I kind of think they do."

"I'm betting on it, but maybe we can get lucky, or maybe we can cause such a stink that the bad guys will make a mistake or someone will roll over for us. While we're doing that, Akira, I want you to break into the Argentine federal police computers. I'm hoping we can catch a break there or come up with a list of suspects. Someone big has to be in on this, I want to know who the major players are down here.''

Tokaido looked up embarrassedly. "Um, Striker?"

"You don't think you can do it?"

"Well, no, busting in should be easy, but once I'm inside, all the files and the commands to get into them are probably going to be in Spanish. I've had two years of Spanish back in high school. I got straight Cs."

"Rafe will help you."

McCarter stretched out the map of South America on the table. "If someone really wants to start a war, there's going to have to be big money involved. They're also going to have to have connections with someone high up in the Argentine military to really get the ball rolling."

"I was reading *La Nacion* on the plane, as well as the *London Times*. The ball is rolling, and you should see the headlines. All the networks talk about is a possible second Falklands war. CNN already has news crews at Port Stanley interviewing the locals. I don't know if the Bear told you, but the U.K. is assembling a naval task force. I've seen the footage. It's all Harrier jump jets and attack helicopters being prepped. Neither government wants a fight, but they both look like they're getting ready for one, and there are no marching bands or brave speeches this time. They both look deadly serious."

Schwarz stared at the map. "When Argentina lost the Falklands war, the military government got thrown out. I'd put money on some members of the old administration having a hand in this."

"Rafe, you're going to have to pull your doctor routine to get us into the city morgue. I want to go in soft. If we go in hard and leave any trace, we could alert the opposition that something is up. Can you do an Argentine accent?"

Encizo smiled smugly. "*Si, Señor Bolan, no problemo.*"

Bolan had seen Encizo go from a Colombian drug lord to a Cuban plantation owner to a Mexican peasant in the space of a single day, but they had never worked this far south before. He smiled and shook his head.

"All right, Rafe, you and I are going to go play medical examiner. Akira, you get your equipment up and running ASAP. David, use the secure line and get ahold of the U.S. Embassy. See if Cecilia is all right and if her mother got out of town. See if she has calmed down."

McCarter raised an eyebrow. "You think we can use her?"

"She speaks Spanish. She knows the town. The bad guys want her dead and want to plunge her country into war with England. If she can pass the gut-check, she might just be able to help us in some way. If nothing else she might be useful translating for Akira when Rafe can't help him."

"You've got it. I'll try to convince her it's her patriotic duty."

"All right, Rafe, let's go try on some doctor's smocks."

THE RIDE TO THE morgue was without incident. While they couldn't use CIA operatives from the embassy in an active field role, they did have access to their inherent talents. Bolan and Encizo had excellent identification that would pass all but the most stringent examination by policemen with access to government files. They passed through El Centro and the towering Obelisk of Argentina. It looked astoundingly like the Washington Monument. The Plaza de Mayo was large with an immense traffic circle surrounding it.

Encizo drove the car through the downtown traffic until they reached the morgue. The identification the CIA embassy staff had created for them cut through the red tape with ease. Encizo did the talking. They soon found themselves in the office of Dr. Tito Lopez. The doctor was a tall man with a mustache. He had an easy smile that contrasted with his sharp eyes, the eyes of a man who spent a great deal of time peering into things.

Lopez peered up at Encizo.

"So, Dr. Molina. I understand you wish to see the bodies from the shooting during the riot?"

"Indeed. I have been asked to look into the matter."

"Ah," Dr. Lopez replied as he led the way from his office down a long hallway. He and Encizo spoke in such rapid Spanish Bolan could understand only half of what they were saying; but the commando had seen the effects of enough violence that he could keep up his end of the conversation with a coroner.

Dr. Lopez suddenly turned to Bolan and shot out a long stream of Spanish. Bolan could tell most of the words were technical terms. He had no idea how to frame an intelligent response. The ball had been fumbled.

Encizo picked it up and ran with it. The soldier spoke in English. "Ah, excuse me. Apparently you weren't informed. Dr. Belasko is an American. He is a doctor attached to the Federal Bureau of Investigations fast-reaction teams. He is part of the federal police's exchange program with the United States."

Dr. Lopez's eyes widened. He spoke in very good English. "I'm very pleased to meet you, and I must admit this is most exciting. I have never met a member of the FBI. What is your specialty, Dr. Belasko?"

Bolan kept up his poker face. "Ballistics."

"Ah!" Dr. Lopez grew animated. "Then you will find this fascinating. I have never seen such shooting in my life. One of the men, a sniper, was taken with a 3-round burst from a 9 mm weapon. The burst walked up his chest to his throat and then to his forehead. Most remarkable. Particularly as it was done with a machine pistol, held freehand against an opponent armed with a rifle on a second-story landing."

"Anything is possible, Dr. Lopez. Practice is the only secret."

Dr. Lopez grinned. "Indeed. A wise saying."

They proceeded down the hall and came upon a young intern reading at a table. He leaped up from his textbooks. "Yes, Dr. Lopez?"

"Lucio, this is Dr. Molina, and Dr. Belasko from the United States Federal Bureau of Investigations. He is here on exchange with the federal police. Our guests wish to review the cases of the men brought in from the shooting at the riots outside the British Embassy."

"I gave the keys to the police inspectors."

"What police inspectors?"

"They came to take the bodies."

"Why was I not informed of this?" Dr. Lopez asked.

"Your signature was on the paperwork."

Dr. Lopez looked at Bolan and Encizo and then back at the intern. "There has been some kind of mistake. When did this happen?"

"Ten minutes ago. I believe the inspectors are still in the morgue."

Bolan smiled outwardly at the confusion. Inwardly he went on full alert. A quick glance at his teammate told him Encizo was thinking the same thing. Dr. Lopez was red-faced. "I'm sorry, there seems to be some sort of mix-up."

Bolan smiled. "You have no idea what a mix-up is until you have worked for the U.S. Federal Government. Think nothing of it. I'm very impressed with your facility."

"You're too kind. Let me look into this."

Encizo smiled. "Let us accompany you. I have many friends among the inspectors. Perhaps I can help."

Bolan and Encizo followed the doctor to an elevator. It went down a floor and then opened into the unmistakable chill of a morgue. The room was the universal gray-blue of all morgues, with overhead fluorescent lighting that threw harsh white light into every nook and recess of the long vault. Six men were in the middle of the room. Two of the "meat lockers" were open and the cadaver trays rolled out. The pale forms of two bodies were visible through thick plastic bagging. Lopez rushed forward.

The men looked up. They had three gurneys for transporting bodies. They didn't seem pleased as Lopez approached. One of them stepped forward and held up the badge he carried around his neck on a chain. "This is official police business, Doctor. These men were involved in crimes against the state. They are to be transferred."

Lopez nodded. "Ah, may I ask on whose authority? I wasn't informed of this." He suddenly looked back at the Stony Man soldiers. "It seems I'm not being informed of many things. However, I don't question your authority, it is simply that I would be remiss in my duties if I didn't see the paperwork and sign it."

The men looked askance at one another. Encizo shot a look at Bolan. The Executioner nodded.

The two of them lashed out.

Bolan took a step forward with his left foot and whirled 360 degrees. His right fist blurred as it swung like a ball and chain and his back-fist took the lead man in the temple. Encizo let out an earsplitting scream and drove his heel into the solar plexus of the man in front of him. Both inspectors dropped as if they had been shot.

The morgue was a vast empty room. There was no cover and they were outnumbered. A blinding offense was the only way to safety. The two soldiers tore into the remaining four men. One man's arm shot across his chest and under his coat for the gun in his concealed shoulder holster. Bolan covered the man's arm with his palm and pinned it. In the split second the man tried to yank his gun arm free, Bolan's stiffened hand rose like a blunt ax and swept down to shatter the man's collarbone. The man screamed and the Executioner rammed both palms into his chest. The crippled inspector flew into the man behind him, and they tripped and fell in a tangle of limbs and upset gurneys.

"Gun!"

Bolan recognized Lopez's voice. Then he saw the Czech Skorpion machine pistol that came out from under the coat of one of the inspectors. He had been on the wrong end of such assassination weapons more times than he cared to recall. Bolan took the only course available.

He leaped straight into the gun.

The killer fired from the hip as Bolan lunged. The ripping snarl of the muzzle blast was deafening in the echoing vault of the morgue. The .32 caliber bullets tore through Bolan's coat and slammed into his stomach. The inspector held down the trigger and the burst walked up Bolan's chest like rapid-fire body shots from a heavyweight boxer. The soldier grimaced as the blows came in. His stiffened fingers thrust forward and into both of the shooter's carotid veins.

The gunman's eyelids fluttered as the twin arteries that serviced his brain and the bundles of nerves beneath them were temporarily crushed. The Executioner slapped the machine pistol out of the killer's hands and drove his knee into his groin. The man doubled, and Bolan seized him by his collar and the back of his belt. Bolan heaved the man face first into the steel door of the meat locker.

The soldier whirled. His sound-suppressed Beretta appeared in his hand like a magic trick.

Encizo had demolished one of the men and had just slammed the remainder against the row of vaults.

Lopez hurtled in low at the man's knees in a perfect soccer tackle. The killer fell on top of the doctor. Encizo strode forward and dislocated the hardman's jaw with his heel. Bolan kept his muzzle trained on the first two men he had dealt with. The first moaned and clutched at his arm, which hung awkwardly from his shoulder. The man beneath him was unhurt. He held his hands out to his sides with the palms up, staring with great concern into the muzzle of Bolan's Beretta.

Bolan's eyes didn't move from his target. "Rafe, are you okay?"

"I'm fine." His voice had a tinge of concern to it. "How are you?"

The adrenaline reaction was beginning to subside. Beneath his Threat Level II soft body armor he could feel the bruising start to rise. The Czech Skorpion machine pistol wasn't a powerful weapon. Its .32 caliber bullets were anemic by modern standards, but the little machine pistol sent them out in swarms. He would have to take off his shirt to find out, but Bolan was fairly sure he had taken nine or ten hits. With one finger he probed the top of his chest. If he had been a split second slower the long burst would have walked up past his armor and taken him in the throat.

Encizo pulled the unconscious killer off Dr. Lopez. He gave the doctor a hand and Lopez rose painfully favoring his hip. Encizo smiled at him. "That was smartly done. Thank you."

Lopez took a step back. He looked at both men. His eyes were very wide, but he spoke calmly. "I would very much like to know what's going on here."

Bolan kept his eye on the man beneath his muzzle. "These men aren't police inspectors."

Lopez nodded thoughtfully. "I believe I agree with you. However, I don't believe that either you or Dr. Molina are doctors."

Encizo shot a look at Bolan. The Executioner jerked his head at the man on the floor. "Cover him."

Encizo drew his .45 and smiled down at the man. Lopez eyed the pistol in Bolan's hand as the Executioner turned. "You have a choice."

Lopez took a step back. Bolan flipped the Beretta's selector switch to safe and holstered it. Lopez relaxed slightly. "Oh?"

"Yes. We can tie you up and leave you with most of these fellows, and we will make a phone call once we leave to send someone downstairs to discover you."

Lopez looked at the moaning and unconscious bodies on the floor and considered being tied up. "What's my other choice?"

"You can help us."

"And just what kind of assistance do you require?"

"Someone is trying to start a war between Argentina and the United Kingdom." Bolan gestured at the fallen men. "I believe that these men work for them."

"I see." Lopez took a deep breath. "May I ask who it is you work for and in what capacity?"

"No. However, I'm here to try to prevent this war."

"I see, and if I don't choose to help you?"

"Like I said, we leave you here. We won't kill you. If you wish to report this matter you're free to do so. But the police will find that we have diplomatic immunity."

Dr. Lopez sighed heavily. "What is it you want me to do?"

**7**

"Are we in?"

"Oh, we're in all right," Akira Tokaido answered. "The Argentine federal police mainframe is nicely set up, decent safeguards, but antiquated. Getting in was a snap. I don't speak much Spanish, but just by the architecture I can guess what each command and response is going to be. Having to use a language dictionary is the only slow part."

"I may be getting you some more help on that," Bolan responded.

"Cool. I'm currently installing some translation software the Bear sent. I should have it up and running soon."

"Can you get into the fingerprint section?"

"I can get into anything you want." Tokaido smiled confidently. "We're ghosts, boss. No one will ever know we were here."

Bolan held out a file. "Scan these into your database, then run them against the police fingerprint library. I want names and rap sheets on them if possible. Run them against the FBI and Interpol databases as well. I want to know who they've worked with in the past, who they've been rumored to work with, political connections, anything and everything."

Bolan turned to McCarter. "What's going on at your end?"

McCarter didn't look terribly pleased. "Not much, I'm sorry to say. British Intelligence has precious little in the way of resources in South America except for a few business contacts in our former colony of Belize."

Gadgets Schwarz stretched his arms. He had spent the day doing nothing except battle jet lag. "So what do we do now?"

"We're heading north."

"To Paraguay?"

"That's where the first boys we met down here are from." Bolan looked at the file in his hand. "Dr. Lopez found records on one of them for us. Arturo Moreno was the man I took out on the stairs. He was accused but never convicted of the kidnapping, rape and torture of an Argentine labor union leader's wife. He ran with some bad people. I have a list here of some of them. I think it's time we paid them a visit and asked a few questions.

"Akira? Do you think you could break into the Paraguayan police computer before noon?"

Tokaido looked vaguely offended. "I can find Butch Cassidy and the Sundance Kid for you if you want."

## Asunción, Paraguay

BOLAN HADN'T BEEN in Paraguay in some time, and it didn't look as if it had changed much. Its people were proud, despite being the poorest in South America. Paraguay had suffered the most in South American history. In 1864 the dictator Solano Lopez plunged Paraguay into a suicidal, three-way war against Argentina, Brazil and Uruguay. Even against such overwhelming odds, the Paraguayan people had fought with remarkable bravery in a war that lasted until 1870. By the time Lopez had finally been surrounded by Brazilian lancers and killed, the population of Paraguay had been reduced from 1.4 million to 220,000. Less than thirty thousand adult males had survived the six-year conflict. Paraguay ceded more than 55,000 square miles of territory to Argentina and Brazil. She lost her seacoast, and her newly landlocked economy had been so badly crippled by the loss of man power and destruction of resources that it still hadn't recovered.

The rented Land Rover rolled out of the big city and into the countryside. The capital city of Asunción was right on the border of Argentina and was the point of influx for large numbers of immigrants. It was also the influx point of a great deal of smuggling and crime as well. The Colombian drug lords had moved a substantial part of the growing end of their operations to the mountains of northern Paraguay.

Encizo held the wheel. "So, we go in hard?"

Bolan nodded. "Seems the best way to go." Dr. Lopez had at first seemed somewhat reluctant to give them information, but when he had used his contacts among the federal police and looked up fingerprint records on his own, he had seen the kind of scum Bolan was interested in and he had lost a great deal of his reluctance.

The ranch they were headed toward belonged to Horace Aigular. Aigular was a local strongman. He specialized in kidnapping and extortion, and with the Colombian drug traffic, he had leaped upward in power. Arturo Moreno was linked to Aigular, but no CIA or Interpol computer file would have had such information. It had taken Lopez's contacts in the Argentine federal police to find rumors to that effect.

Bolan grimaced. Lopez was putting himself in the hot seat. He was doing it of his own free will, but Bolan had no doubt sooner or later someone would be coming for the good doctor.

The sun began to set as they drove on. "How far to the ranch?"

"Twenty miles."

"Park it. We'll walk in."

Encizo took the Rover off the road and stopped behind a stand of trees. Bolan, Encizo, McCarter and Schwarz shrugged out of their civilian clothes and into their black raid suits. Each carried a sound-suppressed 9 mm Colt carbine loaded with heavy, subsonic hollowpoints. Each weapon had an M-203 40 mm grenade launcher slaved beneath the barrel. Each man wore a bandolier of assorted grenades. Encizo looked at the canister he loaded into the breech of his grenade launcher. "I really hate this stuff."

Bolan loaded a similar canister into his own weapon. "I do too. But we have to go in hard and fast. I don't want to light the place, and I want as few gunshots as possible. If Aigular is the big shot around here he's going to have servants and other nonhostiles working for him. I want the entire household down and out without unnecessary casualties."

Night had fallen and the four of them pulled their night-vision goggles down over their eyes. The flatlands of Paraguay lit up in flat shades of gray and green. An occasional cow turned a head to look at the shadows passing through the grass, but other than that they went unseen. Outside of Asunción the stars filled the skies by the thousands, and the Southern Cross shone down on them. A glow filled the horizon in their goggles as they approached a slow roll of hills. As they crested it, the lights of the ranch were dazzling in the amplification of the goggles.

Schwarz swept the land with his binoculars. "We've got dogs on the premises, just like you figured. Big ones, and it's a breed I've never seen."

Bolan raised his own binoculars. There were at least four dogs that he could see. They were snow-white and short-haired. They were big, running at least ninety pounds. "Rafe?"

"They're hunting dogs. Hunters in Argentina bred them specifically to track the wild boar that live in the Andes. They've been known to eat people."

"Bloody hell!" McCarter wasn't pleased.

Bolan's hand went to the pack at his side. Inside it were four tri-tips laced with tranquilizer and swimming in juice. "Will they take the meat with the sedatives?"

Encizo thought long and hard. "Yeah, they'll take it."

"Are you guessing or do you know?"

"They're big and they're nasty, but, like I said, they're hunting dogs, not guard dogs."

McCarter kept his eye on the dogs below. "So, just who is going to sneak up within sniffing distance and toss it at them?"

Encizo grinned in the dark. "You. Striker's in command, I'm the most fluent in Spanish, and we're going to need Gadgets for technical work back in Buenos Aires. That makes you the most expendable."

McCarter was silent for a moment. He had been in fire zones on every continent on earth and faced incalculable odds and come out on top. Being eaten by giant dogs in Paraguay was something the Briton had never given much thought to. "All right. Give me the meat."

Bolan handed him the sealed packet. McCarter licked his finger and held it to the wind. "The wind is blowing from the east. I'll make my way around and then open the packet about a click away."

Encizo considered. "Leave three-quarters of it and then take the last part a few dozen yards back. The dogs should stop at the main meat pile, but they won't let the yappers have any. They'll scamper off if they smell more somewhere else. They should be used to eating at the fringes of the pack."

"Good idea." McCarter moved east through the low hills. The rest of the group shadowed him a hundred yards back. If the plan failed, they would have to shoot the dogs.

McCarter stopped two hundred yards from the house and opened the package. He held it up to the wind and then set it down, hastily retreated and dropped the rest behind him. He didn't run, but he moved swiftly backward to rejoin the group.

They watched as one of the dogs raised his massive head and sniffed the air. Everything depended on how the lead dog would react. If he went into hunt mode and began coursing the pack would follow him and the yappers would start the ruckus.

The big dog's body went rigid as he sniffed the wind again. The other dogs rose. The lead dog moved toward the meat. The tri-tip was in chunks, spread out so that no two dogs would start fighting over a single piece of meat. The yappers moved swiftly and silently past to get the meal that they smelled waiting farther off in the dark.

The dogs swiftly wolfed the meat. Then, one by one they lay on their sides in the grass.

Bolan nodded. "Let's go."

The main house blazed with lights. Two men stood off by a separate garage with shouldered AK-47 rifles, smoking cigarettes as they talked. They hadn't even noticed the dogs leave. The strike team fanned out. Encizo moved toward the two men. Bolan whispered into his throat mike as he moved toward the front door.

"Rafe. Can you hear what they're saying?"

"Yeah. They're saying Aigular has a union leader's wife down in the basement. These two are hoping they get their chance at her before they make her too ugly."

"Take them out."

Encizo's weapon made a soft rushing noise. The laughter and music from inside was much louder.

"Anyone in back?"

McCarter's voice came back in Bolan's earpiece. "Two."

"Take them."

There was a heartbeat's pause. "Both down."

"Gadgets, you find the fuse box?"

"You've got lights-out whenever you want it."

"All right. Everyone get your masks on. Launchers locked and loaded. I want three rounds each. I want maximum dispersal throughout the house."

"Roger. On your command. Ready."

"Gadgets! Lights!"

The lights of the hacienda blinked out. The music cut. A woman screamed.

Bolan raised his aim to the great front window. "Fire!"

Four great thumps split the night and pale yellow fire lit up the grounds around the ranch. Bolan flicked open his smoking breech and loaded another grenade. He aimed at an upstairs window and fired and reloaded again. There was little noise other than the thumps of the M-203s being fired in rapid succession, followed by screams and breaking glass.

Bolan took half a second to check the seal on his gas mask before kicking in the front door. The double doors flew wide. Two men with Uzis lay on the floor in gastrointestinal agony. One of the spent grenades lay on the floor of the wide foyer. It spun lazily in a circle.

Bolan stepped past gingerly to avoid slipping in the mess. Adamsite was a nonlethal riot-control gas, but no sane person would ever want to be exposed to it. It was stronger than tear gas, and it had the unpleasant knockout punch of inducing projectile vomiting. It wasn't fatal, but anyone exposed to it wished it was, and all thoughts of counterhostility left their minds.

Bolan moved swiftly through the house. It was two-story Spanish architecture, with wide landings and open foyers and halls. The twelve grenades they had fired would have saturated the house within seconds. Guards and servants lay on the tile floors retching helplessly. Bolan moved into the main dining room.

The soldier scanned the contorted faces lying around the table. He recognized Aigular from the photo Dr. Lopez had acquired. He grabbed him by the collar and dragged him out toward the dining room's glass doors. Bolan checked his team. "What's the situation?"

"This is David. I have no hostiles standing on the first floor. Continuing sweep."

"This is Rafe. No one but servants are upstairs. Continuing sweep."

"Finish your sweep and come down. I'm going to need an interpreter."

"On my way."

"Gadgets, go downstairs and see if they really have a woman there."

Bolan opened a glass door and threw Aigular to the wooden deck of the patio. He closed the door behind him to keep the gas from dispersing too quickly. Encizo appeared and they both waited for the gas that had escaped onto the patio to disperse. Aigular was fat and balding, his nausea wasn't helping his pasty complexion.

"Gadgets, what have you got?"

Schwarz's voice was grim. "Our friend has a small but well-equipped chamber of horrors down here. The woman is unhurt. She's been beaten, but her clothes are still on. I think the fun was going to start after dinner."

"David, what have you got?"

"Two hostiles came out of the stable. They're down. I've swept the garage. No one there."

"Vehicles?"

"Two Ford F-150s. Two Land Rovers. A Jeep and a Mercedes. Some ATVs and dirt bikes."

"Gadgets, find some keys. Put the woman in a car and get her out of here. Tell her she should get her family out of the capital for a while."

"You've got it."

Bolan pulled off his mask and took a cautious breath. His nose prickled slightly at the acrid odor. Aigular was green and looked rung out but his retching had stopped. Bolan put his foot on his chest and leaned. Aigular wheezed.

"Rafe, translate for me exactly. Tell him I'm going to make him a deal. He'll tell me exactly what I want to know, and will do whatever I ask. If he does this I'll allow him to live."

Encizo looked down at Aigular and spoke in rapid-fire Argentine *Castallano*.

Bolan drew his combat knife. The seven-inch stainless-steel Tanto blade seemed to catch the light of every star above them. "Tell him we have his dogs in our van about a mile down the road. Tell him they are very pissed off at being tricked into our truck and they're tearing it apart trying to get out."

Encizo leered down as he spoke.

"Tell him if he doesn't cooperate I'm going to cut out his tongue, and I'm going to bleed him and feed him to his dogs."

Aigular went from green to white. He began babbling the names of a dozen saints. Bolan leaned hard into his chest and cut him off. "Ask him if he understands. Tell him I want his answer."

Encizo asked him. Aigular nodded rapidly.

"Ask him who paid for his men to make the kidnapping at the embassy dinner."

Aigular was visibly shaken by the question.

"He says he was contacted by men he knew. They had been contacted by someone else. Money had been exchanged. Who really wanted it done was none of his business. That's how these things are done."

Bolan considered that likely. "Tell him he's going to make a phone call to the people he does know. He's going to tell them that there are Americans hanging around Asunción asking questions. Questions about what happened at the embassy in Buenos Aires. He is going to say the Americans claim to be journalists but look like soldiers to him. Then he's going to tell us the names of every associate he has in the Americas, every player he knows, has heard of, and every rumor no matter how ridiculous. Tell him I'm going to watch the dogs eat his balls if he doesn't."

Aigular shrieked.

Encizo smiled. "I think he's eager to cooperate."

**8**

*São Paulo, Brazil*

Waldemar Salome's body was sheened with sweat. His long hair flew as he circled. The drums pounded the rhythm faster and faster and his body moved with it. He studied his opponent as the twanging howl of the single stringed *berimbao* grew in intensity. The musicians and chanters all stood in a circle as Salome and his opponent circled and lashed out at each other. It was the *roda*, the circle, where the deadly game was played. It was a scene that played itself out on street corners throughout the coastal cities of Brazil. Salome had played the art of *capoeira* since he had been old enough to walk. He was a man born with nothing. The dusty streets of Rio de Janeiro had been his training ground. Through *capoeira* he had forged his body and his mind. Endless hours of training had developed his discipline until it was a thing of iron.

*Capoeira* had many levels. To the uninitiated it looked like little more than a dance. To others it was a form of music, a cultural legacy left over from the days of slavery and the traditions brought to South America from Africa. To others it was just another martial art, a beautiful and deadly one to be sure, but nothing more than kicks and blows.

*Malicia* was one aspect of *capoeira*. It, too, had many levels. It could be trickiness in combat or the use of deceptive moves. It could be one's attitude or it could be deliberately evil behavior. *Malicia* in a master was being one whose movements couldn't be predicted in the circle, and even further, one who could predict the movements of others before they happened. True *malicia* was knowing the opponent's mind and defeating him before he ever set foot in the circle.

Developing *malicia* had been the consummate quest in Waldemar Salome's life. It had been the base upon which he had built his empire.

The music played faster and faster. The drums thundered like the great heartbeat of the earth. Salome's opponent slashed his kicks in a whirling attack. The music had built from a slow tempo where both men had hugged the ground and seemed to defy gravity in slow motion. Now the music's speed seemed to be reeling out of control. The display of skill was over. This was a challenge. Both men were trying to land a knockout blow. They spun and cartwheeled, and in every moment and from every posture a foot lashed out to attack.

Both men rose and whirled into spins. They slid into the arcs of each other's attacks. The heel of Salome's opponent missed his jaw by a hair. The edge of Salome's foot struck the side of his opponent's face like an ax.

The man fell without control. His body bounced as it hit the smooth wooden floor, and he lay unconscious. The master of the circle signaled for the halt. The fallen man was carried away.

The *Indios* stood in the back and watched in fascination. Salome had been forced to explain to them repeatedly that in the circle he was as other men, and they couldn't kill the men who struck at him.

Nico Souza stood with the bodyguards. He was one of Salome's most trusted men from his old days running the streets. Salome had been so entranced in the game that he hadn't noticed him enter. Souza wouldn't disturb his practice unless something important was happening.

Salome took a towel and smiled at his oldest friend. "Nico, you should come and practice. You're getting fat."

Souza smiled. His days of physical practice had stopped the day he had first held a gun in his hand. He patted his belly. "Women like a man of substance. That way they know he is successful. Besides, you train enough for both of us, Latigo."

Waldemar smiled. All *capoeiristas* were given nicknames. He had earned the name "the Whip" long ago. "Why are you stinking up my *roda* with your cheap cigars?"

"There is news."

"What?"

"It has come to my attention that there are Americans in Asunción. Aigular says they're asking questions. Questions they shouldn't be asking. Two are posing as journalists, another is pretending to be an Argentine police inspector but Aigular says he doesn't believe it. He says they look like hardmen. Aigular has had them followed. He says his own men have seen them conferring together outside the capital. He says at least one of them has rented a ranch outside of town. The Paraguayan wants to know if you want him to continue to watch them or if he should send some men to kill them."

Salome wiped the sweat from his muscles even as his mind rolled this over. "This is a very interesting development."

"There's more. There is news from Buenos Aires as well."

"Ah?"

"There has been trouble in the city morgue. We weren't able to dispose of the shooters' bodies from the riot."

Salome looked up sharply. "What do you mean?"

"Somehow our men were discovered while they were acquiring the bodies. One of the medical examiners interrupted them."

"Why didn't they just kill him?"

"Apparently he had help."

"What kind of help?"

"Two men, who remain unidentified."

Salome considered this. "We sent six men."

Souza looked uncomfortable. "This is so."

Salome scowled. "How many were killed?"

"None."

"None?"

"It seems the doctor and his two friends defeated our men in hand-to-hand combat. Most of our men sustained serious injuries. All of them are currently in custody."

"I want them bailed out immediately. Then I want them to disappear."

Souza's discomfort grew. "That will be difficult. They're being held on very serious charges. Impersonating police officers, breaking into a federal facility, assaulting the chief medical examiner, possession of unlicensed automatic weapons and obstructing justice. Legally, I don't believe the prosecutor will be able to make the charge of grave robbery stick, but the fact that our men were stealing dead bodies looks bad, very bad. It may be impossible to bail them out anytime soon. I'm certain they'll at least be arraigned before we can do anything to extricate them."

Salome's jaw clenched. With a deliberate effort he made himself relax. "Very well. See that they are killed. Quickly."

"As you say. What do you wish me to do about the situation in Paraguay? Do you want to let Aigular handle it?"

"No. First, who's this medical examiner?"

"A Dr. Lopez. He has a very high reputation."

"His helpers could only have been the Briton and the American."

"From what I have learned, even Dr. Lopez's superiors don't know who these people were. He's in some trouble over this."

"I gather both men have disappeared."

"Yes."

"Have the Briton or the American returned to either of the embassies?"

"No."

"I want this Dr. Lopez watched. I want his house bugged. I believe our opponents may try to use him as a resource."

"I have already done so. What do you wish me to do about the situation in Paraguay?"

"Pick men you trust. Don't expose yourself, but see to it personally."

"As you say."

Salome's mind moved to more important matters. "Where is Ladislao?"

"He is in Tierra del Fuego. I'm expecting him to contact me within the hour. The last I heard, everything was going according to schedule."

"I want nothing to interfere with our timetable. We need to start the next phase."

A thought occured to Salome. "I have changed my mind, Nico."

Souza raised an eyebrow. "Yes?"

"In Paraguay, this is what I want you to do...."

## Tierra del Fuego

LADISLAO DIRAZAR stood on the dock and squinted into the wind and misting rain. It was summer, but summer in Tierra del Fuego meant that the ice and snow had only temporarily been shoved back. He stood on the wharf and looked at the ship's captain before him. The ship had sailed untold thousands of miles to get there. Ushuaia was the southernmost city in Argentina and the southernmost city in the world. It perched on the very tip of South America. The only thing farther south was Antarctica itself.

The ship that stood at dock was a good-sized merchant vessel, capable of taking on large, intermodal container boxes.

The ship looked to be riding low in the water with the weight of what she carried.

The captain was a very large man in a stained peacoat. He had a craggy face and a gray brush cut. His cigarette stank of cheap tobacco. He struck Dirazar as the kind of sailor who had seen a thousand ports of call, and only stayed long enough to see the worst parts of each one as he took on fresh cargo. The captain crushed out his butt on the wet pier and looked Dirazar up and down. He grunted noncommittally. "I'm here."

"You have what we have asked for?"

The captain's Spanish wasn't good. His harsh inflections told Dirazar that he hadn't learned it in South America. "Everything you have asked for and more. You have the money?" He eyed the suitcase in Dirazar's hand.

"You have brought everything?"

The captain looked annoyed. "Yes. I have all the equipment. All the raw materials."

"How are the technicians?"

The captain spit. "They spent half the voyage complaining about their berths. Two of them were of the opinion that the ship runs as a democracy. They had to have the chain of command explained to them."

Dirazar's hand tightened on the suitcase he held. His eyes went hard. "My employer won't be pleased if the men he has paid you to transport are incapable of performing their duties."

"Not to worry," the captain said as he smiled unpleasantly. "I suspect you'll find them to be twice as efficient at following orders as they were previously. You have the money?"

"You received the first installment, I trust."

The captain brightened slightly. "I did. You have the next one?"

Dirazar set down the suitcase. "Do you wish to count it?"

"I'll count it aboard ship. If the sum is incorrect, I'll send your cargo to the bottom of the Atlantic, and your goddamned technicians will be tied to it when I push it overboard.'' The captain smiled, revealing several missing teeth. ''Then I'll come back here and kill you.''

Dirazar smiled. ''I believe you'll be pleased with the sum. My employer has been impressed with your efficiency as well as your discreetness. He has included a personal bonus for you. As for the third installment, it will await you upon final delivery. We can foresee no problems for the final leg of your voyage. It should be clear sailing all the way.''

The captain grunted again, but his eyes betrayed his greed at the word bonus.

Dirazar waited a moment until he realized the captain had nothing else to say.

''Would you mind if I took a look at the merchandise?''

''Suit yourself.''

He followed the captain up the gangplank onto the ship. Despite his disheveled personal appearance, the man ran a tight ship. Dirazar followed him down the narrow corridors. A door opened onto an iron gangway that rose above the main cargo hold. Immense boxes were stacked one on top of the other. Objects that were too big for boxes were covered with huge tarps. Dirazar found himself slightly breathless. Everything was going according to plan. Salome was a genius.

''Is it all here?''

''You want to check the manifest?''

Dirazar shook his head. ''No, that won't be necessary.'' He grinned at the captain. ''Have a safe voyage.''

**9**

*Asunción, Paraguay*

Horace Aigular was as white as a sheet as he set down his phone. "They're coming."

"When?"

"Tonight, at midnight."

Encizo nodded at Bolan. "He told them what we said. They think we're gone, and Aigular and some of his men are waiting here for us to return. Whoever is in command wasn't too pleased, but he told Aigular to wait here."

Bolan examined the wall of the ranch they had rented through Aigular. "Gadgets, can you wire this place before noon?"

Schwarz smiled. "You think our friends might show up a little earlier than expected?"

"I'm counting on it."

"No problem. I wish we had a little more to work with, but I think we can rig up a decent reception for them."

Bolan looked to Encizo. "How are you and your new pals doing?"

"Striker, those dogs are awesome. Absolutely awesome. We've got to get some of these for the Farm." He had spent the morning working with the dogs. He'd had them standing on their hind legs for him and snarling at their former master in minutes. Aigular was horrified. He was still in absolute terror that Bolan was going to make good on his threat.

"Can we count on them?"

"Definitely. They've only had the most basic of training." He shot a disgusted look at Aigular. "And they sure as hell never had much of a command relationship with their master. They've just been sitting on their butts going crazy with nothing to do. It only took me about five minutes to figure out what commands they responded to, and about that long again to get them to respond to me. They love it. I'm telling you, we have some highly motivated mutts here, and they're dying for some proper leadership."

Bolan couldn't help but grin. It had been Encizo's idea to use the dogs as a force multiplier. The soldier had to admit that in a night attack, six ninety-pound dogs who didn't bark would make excellent weapons. "They'll obey you at night?"

"If I give them a target, they'll hit it. I guarantee it."

"All right. Pick your spot. I want you covering the rear of the ranch, and I need you in place before sundown."

"I need each of you to come out for a few minutes when you can spare it and familiarize yourself with the dogs. I need them to recognize each team member as part of the pack. We don't want any mistakes when the fur starts flying."

"McCarter's on watch. Why don't you take the dogs out for a walk and let them fall in love with him."

"You got it."

"Gadgets, let's get this house wired up."

Schwarz opened one of his suitcases. Despite his complaining he seemed to have a full load of surprises with him. "Let's do it."

NIGHT HAD FALLEN as the Executioner waited. He checked his watch. It was 9:45 p.m. Every light in the house was on. Bolan wanted everything looking bright and cheerful.

Encizo's voice spoke in Bolan's earpiece. "Striker, we've got vehicles."

"How many?"

"I've got three pairs of lights. Approximately three clicks up the road."

"How big?"

"The lights are high off the ground. They're trucks of some sort. Striker, they've just cut their lights."

"Keep me posted. David, are you in position?"

"Yes, but I don't see what Rafe does. My angle is blocked."

"Hold tight where you are."

"Holding."

Bolan looked at Schwarz, who was holding two black boxes with red buttons on them. "Gadgets, run a final check."

Schwarz moved through the house and checked their preparations a final time. Bolan's eye landed on Aigular. He spoke in Spanish. "You know what you're going to do?"

Aigular nodded vigorously. "*Si, si.* I know what to do."

"You know what happens if you mess this up?"

Aigular went pale again as Schwarz returned. "Everything is a go."

Encizo's voice came through. "Vehicles approaching. Three of them, two pickups and a van. I've got four men in the back of each truck confirmed. I can't see inside the van. Men in trucks are armed. Automatic weapons of some kind."

"This is McCarter. I can confirm. I've got Uzis and AK-47s in sight. Vehicles are stopping, men deploying. They are fanning out to flank the ranch."

Encizo cut in. "I've got six coming my way."

"Four coming my way. Striker, you've got about twelve moving toward the front of the house. The other two teams are flanking. I count twenty-four hostiles. All armed."

"Twenty-four confirmed, Striker. At least two people are still in the van."

"Roger that." Bolan stood and turned toward his prisoner.

"Aigular, it's time to say hello to your friends. Gadgets, be ready."

Aigular rose unsteadily. His eyes rolled toward the front door of the ranch.

Encizo spoke. "Striker, west-side flanking team has stopped. They have sighted Aigular's trucks. They are conferring among themselves. One of them is using a cellular phone."

McCarter's voice spoke into Bolan's earpiece. "East-side flanking team is holding position. Team leader is on the horn. They're having a conference call."

Bolan rested his M-4 carbine across his knee as he waited, the seconds ticking by. Aigular jumped when his phone rang, then hesitated, gaping at the muzzles of the carbine and the grenade launcher attached beneath its barrel. Bolan jerked his head at the phone. "Answer it."

The Executioner pushed the muzzles into Aigular's side as the man answered the phone.

"*Hola.*"

The voice on the phone spoke rapidly. Bolan could understand enough to know that the man was asking what was going on. Aigular said everything was fine and wanted to know what the hell was going on at the other end. He was quite an actor with his life on the line. The voice told him that he and his men were to step outside, slowly, with their hands in the air.

Aigular looked at Bolan. The Executioner nodded. The Paraguayan stayed on the line as he went to the door. Bolan crouched near the fireplace. Aigular opened the door and stepped onto the front porch.

Gunfire lit up the night. Aigular shuddered backward as he took multiple hits. Schwarz snarled as he dropped to the floor. Automatic weapons fire tore through the doorway and shattered the windows. More weapons opened up and began to tear into the east and west sides of the house. "Nice friends he's got!"

McCarter broke in over the radio. "Striker! I've got headlights! The van is starting to move. It's leaving!"

"Take it out!"

"Roger!" A 40 mm grenade launcher thumped over the noise of the AK-47s. A moment later the unmistakable noise of an anti-armor round detonating melded with the sound of metal being rent. "Vehicle disabled. No one coming out. East-side flanking team has seen me. I'm moving."

Encizo spoke urgently. "Striker. They're charging the house. You've got six moving in the back way."

"Take them out!"

Bullets tore through the open door as a dozen men charged forward firing their weapons. Whoever was in command knew that the best way to break an ambush was to go right down its throat. Bolan rose and fired his M-203. The sound of the 40 mm grenade launcher firing inside the ranch was deafening. The fragmentation round flew through the open door and detonated among the chattering muzzle-flashes. Bolan slapped a fresh grenade into the smoking breech of his weapon and pulled his night-vision goggles down over his eyes. "Gadgets, kill the lights!"

Schwarz pushed a button and the ranch plunged into darkness. Bolan faded back toward the interior hallway. The gunmen kept charging straight in, determined to overwhelm the opposition with sheer numbers and firepower. Bolan fired a burst and took cover. Boots pounded on the porch. The noise of automatic weapons grew deafening as men began to spray the interior of the house.

"Gadgets, I've got seven in the house."

"The rest must be flanking."

"Hit it!"

Schwarz's thumb pushed the detonator button. The Claymore mines set in the entryway and living room of the ranch fired. The four mines were set in different corners of the room to create arcs of cross fire. The explosions filled the air with lethal steel projectiles like giant shotgun shells. Bolan and Schwarz continued to fade back.

"Again!"

Schwarz depressed his detonator again. Outside, the mines set in the long grass exploded. Men screamed as they were caught between the clay walls of the ranch and the merciless hail of buckshot.

"Rafe! What's happening?"

"Your back is clear, but not for long."

The Executioner and Schwarz moved to the back of the house. "We're coming out!"

Bolan went out the back door. Six men were down. The guard dogs had hit the killers before they knew what was happening. Encizo had taken them down mercilessly. He pulled at the dogs' leads and yanked them away from the bodies. Bolan scanned the darkness. The rifle fire had tapered off. A few weapons out front were still firing at the house.

"McCarter, what's your situation?"

"I have three down. Three more have taken cover in some rocks. Fifty yards east of the ranch."

Bolan looked at Schwarz. "Gadgets."

"I'm on it." Schwarz moved to the east corner of the ranch and flipped up the sight of the grenade launcher. The M-203 boomed. A split second later the rocks lit up in an orange flash as the fragmentation grenade detonated. The rifle fire from the rocks ceased. McCarter's voice came over the radio. "I'm flanking. Will check for survivors."

"Roger." Bolan turned to Encizo. "We've still got some unfriendlies hunkered down out front."

"No problem." Encizo disappeared around the western corner of the ranch with the dogs pulling at their leads. "I count four hostiles in the grass."

"Take them."

Encizo's low hiss came over the earpiece. "Attack! Attack!"

Bolan and Schwarz moved east around the house. Three men lay dead where the mines had taken them. As they swept to the front, they heard the screaming begin out in the grass along with the furious snarling of the dogs. Bolan moved out at a run. Men and dogs were rolling and thrashing in the grass. The gunmen had been lying prone when the dogs had leaped on them. The men screamed and rolled as the dogs savaged them.

Encizo's voice boomed out at parade-ground decibels. "Stop! Stop!"

The dogs reluctantly pulled back from the bloody gunmen and sat in the grass baring their teeth at them.

"Come!" The dogs came and Encizo scooped up their leads. Bolan and Schwarz kicked away the gunner's weapons.

"McCarter, what have you got?"

"Three in the rocks. All dead. I'm currently sweeping the vehicles. No one is in the trucks. I'm checking the van for survivors."

"Roger. Keep me posted." Bolan looked at the gunmen. "Hog-tie this bunch." McCarter's voice came back through the earpiece. "Striker, I have a survivor, and something else that might interest you."

Bolan turned to Schwarz. "Get the lights back on. Let's see what we have here."

They dragged the survivors back into the house and Schwarz restored the lights. The ranch had been chopped to pieces and bullet strikes pocked the clay walls like a beehive. The survivors were led to the living room. The dead bodies of their confederates were everywhere. The remaining gunmen sat and bled through their bandages. They were torn between staring at their captors and avoiding eye contact. Bolan and his team had pulled black balaclavas over their faces. The sight of the heavily armed masked men in black suits and body armor didn't fill the defeated killers with confidence. They didn't like the fact that Encizo stood a few feet away holding the dogs by their leads. Encizo's control of them was iron. The dogs sat where he had told them to sit, and probably would have stayed there until doomsday unless ordered otherwise. Still, they bared their teeth and growled low at the slightest movement of the gunmen.

It was obvious to everyone the dogs wanted another crack at them.

McCarter came walking in with a captive. The man's clothes were smoke-stained and bloodied but at one time they had been very expensive. He was covered with a great deal of blood but his lacerations looked superficial. His eyes were raccooned with bruising and his nose was broken from where his face had met the dashboard of the van.

McCarter shoved him down onto the couch next to his confederates.

"Who is he?"

"He won't say."

"Where's he from?"

"He won't say that either."

"Rafe."

Encizo gave the dogs a foot of leash. They were instantly off their haunches and snarling at the newcomer. The man flinched away and let out a stream of obscenities. Encizo nodded to himself. "Most of these boys are Paraguayan." He nodded accusingly at the newcomer. "Our friend here is Argentine."

McCarter reached into a fanny pack attached to his web gear. "He had a telephone on him, and I found another on the floor of the van. They have presets and callback."

Bolan smiled under his balaclava. Criminals loved cellular phones. Calls made on them were immensely hard to trace. Many of them only had limited range and were useless if captured.

Bolan turned to Schwarz. "We need to get these phones back to the Farm ASAP. Tell the Bear we're going to need to amplify a microwave signal and bounce it across the equator. Tell him to get hold of Brognola. We're going to need the cooperation of the Pentagon. We're going to need a satellite that's looking down on South America. Tell him I want a full code-breaking suite attached to it in case these guys are smarter than we think, and whatever trace we use is going to have to be powerful and fast. I doubt they'll stay on the phone long and we have to count on them vanishing once they get the call."

"You got it."

Encizo jerked his head at the gunmen. "What do we do with them?"

"Leave them outside. We torch the ranch and leave the guns for the cops to find when they investigate the fire."

"No, I mean what do you want me to tell them?"

"They must tell us everything they know or think they know."

The man from the van began snarling and speaking rapid Spanish. Bolan frowned. He didn't like the defiant tone the man was taking. "Did I hear him ask for a lawyer?"

Encizo nodded. "Oh yeah. He wants his lawyer. He wants a judge. He says he wants all our badge numbers."

Bolan smiled. "Tell him he can have a ten-second running start."

Encizo told him. The man looked back at him blankly. Encizo gave the dogs another foot of slack and they immediately lunged the extra distance. The man screamed shrilly and curled into a ball as they snapped their jaws inches from him. All of the men on the couch began screaming.

Encizo smiled. "It's hard to tell with all of them screaming at once, but I believe they wish to cooperate."

## 10

## São Paulo, Brazil

Waldemar Salome sat drinking fruit juice in his mansion. The news from Dirazar had been good. The merchandise had been delivered. The shipment had gone on. He had just received news that it had reached its final destination without mishap. Construction was already well underway. Everything was going according to plan. Very soon, the little games of assassination and whispering in the dark would end, and the real game would begin. Soon the world would be changed forever.

He turned his gaze to the geopolitical map of the world that filled the entire wall of his private study. His eyes fell upon the United Kingdom. His lips curled slightly. England was a tired old country. Once, she had rightfully boasted that the sun never set upon her empire. Now England was a kingdom in little more than name only. Very soon she would be struck a blow from which she would never recover.

His eyes slid to Argentina. That nation was the greatest waste in the world. She had the resources to feed the world, to power it, to own a great deal of it and exert dominance over much of the rest of it. She should own South America. Even without a nuclear arsenal, she should be a superpower. Instead, she languished like the rest of South America with a tiny, rich elite, a small middle class and a vast horde of the poor; and she was in much better shape than most of the countries south of the equator. Salome smiled. It was time for the situation to change.

Nico Souza entered the room past the bodyguards and looked at his old friend. "You seem satisfied."

"I'm not yet satisfied, but I'm pleased with our progress."

Souza smiled. They had grown up on the same streets, but Salome spoke like a man who had received extensive education. It pleased Souza that his friend was a genius. "As you say."

"Speaking of progress, any news from Paraguay?"

"Our contact in Asunción used a man named Ramon Salcido. He says there was quite a struggle. Aigular was killed. So were a number of our men and Aigular's. The ranch was burned."

"What did they find?"

"Four men."

"Did they match the description of those we seek?"

"Two of them did. The Briton and the American."

Salome's eyes narrowed. "What of the other two?"

"One was Hispanic, the other a white man."

Salome found himself smiling.

"Now are you satisfied?"

"No." Hard won instincts of survival spoke to Salome. "I want their deaths confirmed. I don't know this Ramon personally, and our contact hasn't seen the bodies yet, has he?"

"No, he hasn't. However, Ramon has asked about this himself. He said the bodies were starting to stink, so he ran them through a stump grinder, along with his own casualties and those of Aigular, and our friend Aigular as well."

"What?" Salome sat up in his chair as his suspicions flared.

"However, Ramon seems to have taken the precaution of removing their heads and hands and packing them in Aigular's meat locker. He wants to know who he should give them to. Our contact didn't wish to make the move without your say-so.''

Salome snorted. "We may have to promote this man, Ramon.''

*Asunción, Paraguay*

MACK BOLAN and Ramon Salcido watched CNN. The news correspondent stood on the deck of *Illustrious*. The wind ruffled the woman's hair and she held her ears as a fighter shrieked off the carrier's ski-jump launch deck. The jet tore into the air. She gestured starboard. Off in the distance steamed the *Illustrious*'s sister ship, the *Ark Royal*. The British carriers were small compared to the gigantic floating cities fielded by the United States, but the twin carriers' capabilities couldn't be denied. Each carrier had eight Hawker Sea-Harrier jump jets and an assortment of helicopters, and the carriers didn't sail alone. Broadsword-class frigates patrolled the dark waves of the Atlantic. Bolan also knew that out in the darkness below the waves, Trafalgar-class nuclear-powered hunter-killer submarines stalked the depths.

The British fleet was sailing for the South Atlantic.

Similar preparations were being made in Argentina, though, as yet, no ships had been deployed. Newspapers and newscasters called upon generals and military journalists to conduct endless debates over the size and capabilities of the two fleets. Las Vegas was taking odds on the outcome of a war that grew ever more certain.

It was a war Bolan was determined to prevent. He looked over at Salcido. He was an Argentine national and a career criminal. He was the Argentine front man for a fairly powerful Paraguayan gang. The Argentines funneled in money and guns, and the Paraguayans did the messy work on their own soil. Salcido wouldn't normally have been present except that he had been told to see to the job himself. Bolan had to give Salcido some credit, he had launched a halfway decent assault on the ranch.

He locked gazes with the Argentine. "Ready?"

Salcido nodded unhappily. It was time for him to make a phone call.

"All right, let's set up the link."

Gadgets Schwarz began flipping switches in the two aluminum suitcases that contained the link and the dedicated electronic warfare equipment. He spoke into a microphone. "Bear?"

"Reading you loud and clear." The link to the Farm was established.

"Are we ready on your end?"

"Your satellite window is open. We're prepared to receive your signal, boost it and track it."

Bolan picked up a cellular phone. It had been totally gutted and then reassembled. Wires trailed down from it like spaghetti to the communications gear. Encizo spoke to Salcido in Spanish. "Make the call."

Salcido took the phone and pressed the automatic Redial. The phone signal went directly into the satellite link and was transmitted into space. Six hundred miles above the earth's surface the signal was received by a U.S. military electronic intelligence satellite. The satellite then transmitted the signal back down to the closest local radio relay station. The phone's signal was now on its original path, and the electronic eyes of the satellite were following that path very intently.

The phone rang once, then twice. Both Bolan and Encizo wore headsets that would let them both hear and speak on the line if it was necessary. Schwarz stayed on the equipment. McCarter kept his 9 mm Colt submachine gun pointed unerringly at the Argentine's head. The line picked up on the third ring.

The voice on the other end spoke in Spanish. "Yes?"

Up in space, the satellite's onboard computer began computing the angles of transmission that it was sending and receiving.

"It's me, Ramon."

Back in Virginia, Kurtzman's own computer network was receiving the satellite's triangulation data. It took the coordinates and began comparing them with aerial photographs. Kurtzman's voice spoke in Bolan's earpiece. "The other party is in Asunción."

The voice on the other end of the line sounded distinctly irritated. "Why are you making contact?"

Encizo quickly scrawled a note and held it up for Bolan to read:

He's Brazilian. I can tell by his accent.

Salcido's eyes darted from one to the other and then went back to the muzzle of McCarter's carbine. Ramon didn't need to fake the nervousness in his voice. "Listen, what do you want me to do with these heads?"

"Why are you so concerned? I said you'd be contacted."

Salcido glanced down at the cues Encizo had scripted for him. "I'm telling you, they're starting to make me nervous. You didn't see these men. They wore black uniforms and body armor. It took a dozen bullets to kill each one of them. They had machine guns with grenade launchers and goggles that let them see in the dark. We had total surprise, and they still killed half of my men and almost all of Aigular's. They have boxes and boxes of electronic gear I don't understand. Listen, I'm not stupid. They aren't narcs. They have to be FBI or CIA, maybe even something worse. Maybe Navy SEALs or something. I don't like the idea of sitting here waiting for black helicopters full of their friends to show up. I don't think they'll be pleased to find that I have their friends' heads in a meat locker."

In Virginia, Kurtzman's computer took the coordinates and

laid them across the aerial map of the Paraguayan capital. The computer then called up an extensive map of Asunción's streets and laid the numbers from the aerial map on top of them.

The voice on the other end controlled its irritation and spoke reasonably. "Listen, I hear what you're saying, but no black helicopters will come. They would have to get permission from the governments of Paraguay, Brazil or Argentina to do so. Our contacts say they didn't have permission to be in Paraguay in the first place. Whoever sent them is wondering what the hell happened and how they are going to explain it to their superiors. Their mission is a wash, whatever it was. Right now they are probably trying to cover their tracks, hoping to avoid an international incident with Paraguay. You're safe as long as you do nothing stupid. Sit tight, do nothing. You will be contacted."

Salcido checked his notes. "You are right, but I still don't like sitting here."

"You don't have to like it. Just do it."

"All right, all right. I'm doing it. I'll sit tight and wait for your call."

"Good."

The line clicked off. Schwarz was grinning. Bolan felt relief. It was almost always a good sign when Schwarz appeared insufferably pleased with himself. "What have we got?"

Schwarz adjusted his microphone. "Bear, what have we got?"

"I'm faxing it now."

The fax machine in one of the suitcases began to make a small noise. A sheet of paper began to roll out. It was a close-up of a city map of Asunción. A second sheet came out with a close-up of an aerial map. Both maps were of the same area. Kurtzman sounded pleased with himself. "We have it narrowed down to an area within two blocks."

Bolan peered at the maps. It was a hell of a good job, but a thousand people could live and work within two blocks, and that was assuming the person on the other line was going to stay there for any length of time. "Is there any way we can narrow it farther?"

Schwarz hadn't lost his grin yet. "Striker, the satellite tracked the area by computing the angle between our telephone and the other line in Asunción. The closer we get, the tighter that angle will be and the more precise the coordinates."

"So we go there and make another call."

The electronics expert nodded. "If we can get within those two blocks and make another phone call, and, if our party is still there and picks up, we can get the exact location."

Bolan pulled off his headset. "Let's roll."

## 11

Bolan looked at the house. Dusk had fallen in Asunción. It had taken them a half hour to pack their gear, get back into the capital and locate the area. It was residential, in neither a particularly good nor bad part of town. The house sat on the corner of a street. Aaron Kurtzman was ninety-nine percent sure that it had to be that house or the next one. Ramon Salcido's second phone call had helped pinpoint that one. The party on the other end of the line had been very angry with Salcido. A third call was very likely to cause suspicion. Bolan scanned the other house. They were in the middle of Paraguay's capital city. They couldn't afford a screwup. They sure as hell couldn't afford a firefight. They had to get it right the first time or not at all.

Bolan spoke into his throat mike. "Gadgets, I think we're going to need a third phone call."

Schwarz was in the rented Land Rover half a block down the street. "I don't know. Ramon is supposed to wait for contact, and he's already called twice in one hour. It could raise a stink."

"Going in hard to the wrong house could cause a bigger one."

"You think they'll answer a third call?"

"I think so. Our mysterious friend was pretty pissed off when Ramon made his second call. I believe he's getting the idea that Ramon is going chicken on him. I'm betting if we call again, whoever picks up the phone is going to give our friend a royal ass-chewing.''

"Or he might not pick up at all and call someone else instead to say something is wrong.''

"That's within the realm of possibility.''

"Well, I'll drop the quarter if you want to make the call.''

Bolan scanned both houses. "We're going to try the first house. David, you and Rafe take the front door. When the phone picks up, you knock. If it's our boy we'll hear the interruption. I'll go in the back. If you can't get them to open the door, go in hard, but make it as quick and as quiet as you can.''

"Roger that. We're moving into position.''

Bolan walked around the corner. He was dressed in civilian clothes and carried a newspaper in his hand. He wore Threat Level II body armor beneath his dress shirt and the Beretta with attached sound suppressor rode at the small of his back, concealed by his jacket. He walked casually toward the back of the house. Like much of South America, people came home late, ate dinner late and then went out around midnight. Nine in the evening was an excellent time of day for clandestine activities.

Bolan waited for a passing car to roll by. As its lights flashed past he vaulted the fence and dived into the shrubs. He hunkered down and followed the line of the foliage almost right up to the porch and the back door. There was a light on over the door. Above the porch was a tiny wooden portico with an open window. Its drapes fluttered in the breeze. Bolan moved into the shadows by the tiny landing of the back porch.

"I'm in position.''

"This is Rafe. We're in position.''

"This is Gadgets. The Farm says they're ready on their end, and we still have the satellite window for another twenty minutes. My gear is up and running. Say the word.''

"All right. Make the call. I'll talk through my microphone.

Rafe, if the Bear says it's a go, you knock on the door. You have a story?"

"How about, 'Open up! Police!' They'll have to answer, and it will be less suspicious than playing pizza boy. If it's the wrong house, we just say sorry and move on."

"Good, do it. Gadgets, you ready?"

"Ready."

"Drop the quarter."

The phone picked up on the first ring. Bolan could easily understand the Spanish.

"Goddamn it! Are you a little girl? What the hell is wrong with you? You've been told!"

Bolan replied in Russian.

The voice on the other side choked in surprise and then grew angry again. "Who the hell is this?"

Bolan spoke a few more words in Russian and then spoke in Spanish. "What do you mean who is this? Who are you?"

Kurtzman's voice overrode the angry reply in his ear. "The transmission angle is nearly zero. Ninety-nine percent probability that the other transmitter is in the house. We have a go!"

Bolan could hear the banging on the door at the front of the house. Encizo's voice spoke out in Spanish. He could hear it from outside the house as well as over the other party's receiver. "Police! Open up!"

The voice on the phone was livid. "Miguel! See what the hell the fools want!" The voice returned its attention to the phone. "You, who is—"

"Sorry, wrong number." Bolan hung up and moved swiftly to the porch. He leaped and grabbed the railing. The thin wooden beams creaked but held his weight. The soldier swung his leg up and shot out his arm to grab the windowsill. Bolan drew his Beretta and snaked through the open window.

It was a bedroom, and currently unoccupied. Bolan moved to the door and listened. Below he could hear voices at the door. He opened the door silently and stepped out into the upstairs hallway. The angry voice was growing louder. Whoever Miguel was, he had little fear of the Paraguayan police. He was swearing a blue streak at Encizo.

Bolan flattened himself against the wall as a door opened in front of him.

A large man strode out. He was bare-chested and not wearing shoes. A Browning Hi-Power semiautomatic was thrust into the front waistband of his slacks. He carried a cellular phone in his hand. He craned his head as he listened to the commotion below. He opened his mouth to speak when he suddenly noticed Bolan out of the corner of his eye.

"Hey! What—"

Bolan lunged like a swordsman. The black muzzle of the Beretta machine pistol's suppressor tube punched into the man's solar plexus. The man's knees and elbows pulled in like a crushed spider and his face twisted in strangled agony. Bolan's arm recoiled from the blow and lashed out again in a flat arc. The steel slide of the Beretta 93-R cracked across the man's temple. The Executioner hooked the man under both arms as his knees buckled under him and lowered the unconscious man to the ground.

The door at the end of the hall opened. A tall thin man saw Bolan and went for the revolver riding openly in his shoulder holster. The Executioner twisted his arm out from under the unconscious man and shoved forward the Beretta. The thin man's revolver came free and Bolan fired three quick rounds. The man jerked as the bullets hit him. The cough of the Beretta was nearly silent beneath the voice of Miguel shouting below. The three spent brass shell casings from Bolan's pistol had ejected high into the air and bounced against the wall. The thin man fell face first in the hallway with a thump. For a split second the voices below went mute.

Downstairs, suppressed 9 mm pistols began chuffing in rapid semiautomatic fire. Bolan rose and quickly began to make a room-to-room sweep of the upstairs. Below, the soldier heard a thump and a scraping noise. Then the front door closed. Bolan cleared the upstairs and spoke quietly into his throat mike. "Upstairs is clear. One hostile dead. One down and unconscious."

"Roger that. Rafe and I have three down in the foyer. All dead. We're sweeping the rest of the house."

"Roger. I'm coming down with the prisoner."

Bolan went back to the unconscious man and scooped up his phone. He grabbed the big man's arm and heaved him into a fireman's carry. Bolan grunted as he lugged the big man down the stairs. McCarter had positioned himself by the front drapes and was peering out. "I don't see any reaction on the street. The action went down quietly, but someone had to have heard the yelling."

"We're moving out, now. Gadgets, bring the car around." Schwarz's voice spoke from down the street. "On my way."

"Rafe, find a shirt or a jacket to put on our friend here."

Encizo went to a closet and pulled out a coat. The two of them shrugged it onto the unconscious man. His left eye was swollen shut and he had a goose egg-sized lump on his temple. Encizo pulled open his eyelids one at a time and peered at his pupils. "I don't see any signs of concussion. Other than a hell of a headache, he should be all right when he wakes."

Schwarz's voice came over the radio. "I'm out front. Some people standing on the porch one house down are looking at your position."

"Roger that." Bolan pulled one of the big man's arms around his shoulder. "McCarter, give me a hand. Rafe, take care of the spectators."

Encizo opened the door and went into the yard. Bolan and McCarter carried the big man out to the sidewalk and stuffed him into the Land Rover. Encizo stood in the front yard and boldly waved his fake ID. "This is a police matter. Please, go back into your home!"

The people stared at Encizo for a moment and then reluctantly went back inside. Bolan and McCarter stepped into the car and a moment later Encizo joined them. Bolan nodded at Schwarz. "Drive."

LADISLAO DIRAZAR squinted as the wind tried to pull tears from his eyes. His orders had changed and he had stayed with the ship's captain and followed the cargo to its final destination. The ship's twin cranes had been unloading the container boxes for the past few days. The construction crews had already been at work for several weeks paving the way for the cargo's arrival. A few hundred yards inland huts had been erected for living quarters and a hardier building of concrete had been built to house the more sensitive technical equipment. A helicopter pad had been leveled and demarcated in blazing orange paint. An Aerospatiale Dauphin helicopter sat on the pad and a concrete shed nearby held its fuel. Dirazar was very pleased with the progress. It all looked extremely professional.

One of the technicians continued to babble at him. Dirazar was forced to use the captain as an interpreter. "What's he saying?"

"He says the equipment all checks out. No problems have arisen from transportation or unloading. All that's required is final positioning and then a final check of all systems."

"How soon can everything be ready?"

The captain spoke to the technician in his own language. Dirazar was pleased to see the technician was smiling.

The captain shoved his hands into his pockets and fished out a package of cigarettes. "He says he wants to check all the components again and then run a complete practice scenario."

"Fine. I understand, but how long until everything is operational?"

The captain and the technician spoke for several moments. The captain shielded his lighter and lit his cigarette. "He says to really do a thorough job and check all the equipment will take until sundown. He says he can do the dry run tonight. That will be done on computer to see if all the systems are working together correctly. He says he can be ready for a live test tomorrow morning."

Dirazar's eyes widened. "We can be ready tomorrow?"

The captain shrugged and blew smoke. "That's what he says."

The technician grinned at Dirazar and spoke. Dirazar smiled back. "What did he say?"

"He says he wants to know if you'll have a target in mind by tomorrow."

**12**

*São Paulo, Brazil*

Waldemar Salome sat in darkness. His practice hall was empty. He sat cross-legged on the floor. In his hand he held a telephone. He spoke with his most trusted assassin. The killer had single-handedly kicked off the chain of events that were now inevitably leading to war. The assassin killed with almost complete impunity, and there was no one on earth Salome trusted more.

The killer spoke. "What do you want me to do?"

"There has been trouble in Paraguay. I'm still not sure of the extent of it."

"Is the American dead?"

"At first I was led to believe so, now I'm not so sure."

"So, what is it you wish me to do?"

"I need to go to the south. I wish to oversee our business there personally. I want this business with the American and his associates cleaned up before I come back."

"Who shall be in charge while you're gone?"

"Nico."

"Ah. How do you want me to kill the American?" The assassin paused before adding, "Why not let me do it my way? Before he dies I'll find out everything he knows."

Salome considered that. Ideally, he would like it done that way—the American lured to some secure place and drugged. When the American awoke he would find himself naked and tied. Then the knife would come out and the screaming would begin. Slowly and with extreme precision every secret the American held in his mind would be carved out of him through his flesh.

"No. I don't want to take any chances. Simply kill him at the first available opportunity."

There was a moment of disappointed silence.

Salome's tone lowered a notch. "Am I understood?"

"Yes, it shall be as you wish. The American dies at the first opportunity. What about this Dr. Lopez, the medical examiner?"

"What about him?"

"He's working for the American. He's using his contacts within the police department. Our contacts say he's asking many questions about the men we have used in Argentina."

"What's the status of the men who were captured in the morgue?"

"They're in custody. Bail can't be arranged."

"Have they talked?"

"No. They're sitting tight."

"Kill them."

"I've already made such arrangements. They'll be dead before dawn."

Salome considered the situation. "Even if they speak, these men can't be tied to us."

"Dr. Lopez is also running lists of high-ranking criminals in South America. Names he shouldn't have been able to get from his own contacts."

"I wasn't aware of this."

"Indeed, Dr. Lopez appears to be a clever man. He is making his inquiries quietly, and discreetly. But how is he acquiring such a diverse list of our hirelings?"

Salome already knew the answer. "The American."

"Indeed, and how is the American getting hold of them?"

"Someone is rolling over on us."

"Who could that be?"

Salome's mind was in the circle. He could see his enemy as a shadow, feinting and dodging around him, actively trying to create the opening from which to strike. He knew the answer. Aigular had failed. Salcido had failed. The American was alive and he was crawling up the chain of command like it was a ladder to find his target. "The American is alive. He was last seen in Paraguay. We have committed substantial assets there." Salome's voice turned grim. "We must now assume all assets there have been compromised."

"What do you wish me to do?"

"You won't worry about it. I'll give a list of names to Nico. He'll send men he trusts and kill anyone in Paraguay the American hasn't gotten to yet. You'll do as we have agreed. The American will return to Argentina. I'm sure of it. When he does, you will kill him."

"And what of Dr. Lopez?"

"Kill him, too."

*Asunción, Paraguay*

SIMON MATTOS avoided the big American's eyes. He was in a trap. Salcido, Aigular and his men had given in and told everything they knew at the threat of being fed to dogs. If someone had told Mattos this in conversation he would have laughed. When he tried to meet the cold gaze of the American with defiance it no longer sounded so silly. He wouldn't have believed just four men could have taken Aigular's crew and then Salcido's strike force six hours later. Mattos believed it now with utter certainty. They had gone through his hand-picked bodyguards as if they hadn't existed. He didn't believe the American would have fed anyone to the dogs. Bloodied, beaten and already savaged once, he could see how Salcido and his men might have entertained the idea as creditable. He was still furious with them for having rolled over, but that fury was on the back burner. There were more important issues.

The American had reached out and found him.

This was impossible. Aigular didn't know his name. Salcido didn't know his name. They were street soldiers, and to them, Mattos was a voice over the phone. A voice that gave orders and made their offshore bank accounts in the Cayman Islands magically grow zeros. He was a shadow. A ghost. Sweat ran down Mattos's brow. The point was academic. The American had reached out and pulled him to earth where he was vulnerable.

His immediate survival was a much more important issue.

Mattos sat on the chair with his hands cuffed in front of him. He reached forward with his manacled hands and took a sip of coffee. The cup shook as he sipped. The American watched him. His mouth smiled vaguely but his eyes were as cold as ice. Mattos cleared his throat with some effort.

"May I have a cigarette?"

The American nodded his head at one of his men. The rest of them wore black masks over their faces. The American wasn't bothering, and this bothered Mattos a great deal. A masked man came forward and shook a cigarette from a pack he had rummaged out of a bag. Mattos paled. He had never met Aigular, but he knew his personal habits intimately. The pack with the blue stripe down the side was Aigular's favorite brand of powerful, unfiltered Turkish cigarettes.

The pack was smeared with blood. The masked man shook out several bloodstained cigarettes and discarded them before he found an untainted one. "Here. This one looks okay."

The man lit the cigarette for him and went back to pointing his submachine gun at him.

Mattos nearly choked on the Turkish tobacco. He coughed around the cigarette and looked back at the American. The big man was regarding him frankly. "Simon, we need to talk."

Mattos worked up his courage. "I'd like to talk with my lawyer."

The big man shrugged. "You're not under arrest."

"Oh." Simon found the information very uncomforting. "May I leave?"

"After we talk." Mattos tried to come up with something to say, but the big man cut him off. "Listen, Simon. You're dog dirt as far as I'm concerned, but I don't give a damn. You're not who I want. Let's cut the crap. I want names— who you work for, who you know…"

Mattos cleared his throat again. "And if I cooperate?"

"I'll let you go."

"And if I don't?"

"I'll let you go."

Mattos blinked.

"Who do you work for, Simon?"

Mattos searched for a response.

"You don't have to tell me immediately, Simon, but think about who you work for. Think very hard about your employer and his business practices for a moment. You've been captured. Let's say I drop you off handcuffed and not wearing any shoes in front of the police station in Asunción. What happens to you?"

Mattos knew the answer immediately. He had been compromised. It wouldn't matter whether anyone believed he had kept silent or not. He was a liability. He was a dead man. He choked on his cigarette.

"Here, let me take that for you." The big man took the cigarette and ground it out. "Now, on the other hand, you can tell me what I want to know. I happen to have over a hundred grand of Aigular's money in the bag over there. I'm going to stop this war your friends are trying to start and then I'm going to take your friends down hard. Now, a hundred grand isn't a fortune, but it's enough to lay low until I finish my work. I'll even arrange it so you can get a real quiet head start on disappearing without exposing yourself. I really believe it's in your best interest to help me on this one. I'll give you five seconds to make up your mind."

Mattos took two. "I'd like to cooperate."

"Who do you work for?"

"I don't know who really runs the organization."

"I understand that, Simon, but who do you answer to, specifically?"

Mattos went pale and felt nauseous, but it was from more than just the Turkish cigarette smoke.

The big man folded his arms across his chest. "Simon, let me put it to you this way, if I drop you off in your underwear in Asunción, who do you believe is going to order your death?"

Simon's guts twisted with fear. He felt like throwing up as he uttered the name. "Nico Souza."

**13**

*Deception Island, Antarctica*

Waldemar Salome looked out to where the waves broke on the icebound shore and then to the horizon. The Falkland Islands lay almost exactly a thousand miles due north from where he was. The desolate rock he stood upon had been fatefully christened Deception Island by the original British explorers who had first mapped it. The island lay fifty miles north of Graham Land, which formed the spindly arm of the Antarctic peninsula. The island spent most of the year surrounded by pack ice, and only briefly did the ice break apart and make it a true island, rather than a windswept rock sticking out of Antarctica's seemingly endless snowy terrain.

Salome turned his binoculars to gaze across the dark blue Antarctic waters. He raised his radio into his parka. "Do we have target acquisition?"

There was hardly any static on the line. Salome strongly believed in Japanese covert-communications technology. "Yes, we have the target in sight."

"Transmit target coordinates."

"Yes, at once."

Salome turned and looked at the concrete command shack. One of the men inside held a radio in his hand and waved through the window as he spoke into it. Spanish wasn't his primary language, and he spoke with the harsh inflections of someone who had learned his Spanish from Cubans. "We're receiving target coordinates. All is in order. Setting search and target-acquisition parameters.''

Salome waited patiently as the minutes crawled by.

"Parameters of target area are loaded into the missile's guidance computer. Target acquisition and search parameters are set. Do you wish to initiate the launch sequence?''

"Initiate.''

"Initiating launch sequence. I suggest you put on your goggles and hearing protection.''

Salome was already wearing his polarizing goggles against the wind, but he pulled his hearing protectors up from around his neck and plugged the microphone into one of the earpieces. "Are you still reading me?''

"Loud and clear. Launch sequence initiated.''

A warning Klaxon began honking. Below, yellow warning lights began flashing. Three hundred yards beyond the compound a huge column of dark olive metal began rising on its launch rails to point into the sky. It was over sixty-five feet long and over five feet in diameter. The launch rails locked at a ninety-degree angle.

The man in the shack spoke excitedly. "Ten seconds to ignition! Ten…nine…eight…''

Salome felt goose bumps along his arms and legs. Success or failure was about to be determined.

"…three…two…one…ignition!''

The huge quad nozzles beneath the cylinder spewed white fire. Superheated smoke and flame obscured the ground as the metal column seemed to slide upward in slow-motion along its launch rails. The whole island trembled with the thundering roar and Salome squinted against the glare through his dark goggles. He felt the same giddiness he had first known when as a five-year-old, he had held a match to the fuse of a bottle-rocket on Independence Day.

Destiny roared into the Antarctic sky on a column of fire.

*Drake Passage*

CAPTAIN ALEJANDO VITAL stood on the bridge of the Chilean navy destroyer *Capitan Prat*. The 5,440-ton ship had left the naval base at Punta Arenas at dawn the day before and undergone maneuvers in the maze of island channels that formed Cape Horn. The *Capitan Prat* had made her way out of the channels and was in the open ocean that straddled the line between the Pacific and the Atlantic Oceans. There had been no icebergs of any size worth reporting. No Argentine warships were in the area. There hadn't been a war with Argentina in many years, but there had been a few military buildups and saber rattling along the long border they shared. Much of that border was still in legal dispute. It always made Vital a little nervous when an Argentine warship and his own ship slid by one another. However, there had been no Argentine warships this day. There had been no Antarctic cruise ships or research vessels. Other than a pod of whales, the maneuvers had been routine.

"Captain."

Vital turned to his electronics warfare officer. "Yes?"

The young lieutenant shook his head. "Sir, I have a very strange reading."

"What is it?"

"It's very odd, we seem to be detecting some kind of active homing radar. It's in search mode."

There was nothing with a search radar within a thousand miles. The captain was sure of it. "From where?"

The lieutenant frowned at his screen. "I can't be sure."

"Are there any surface ships within radar range we should know about?"

"No, Captain. None we have been apprised of."

Icy chills ran down the captain's spine. There was only one explanation. There was a submarine somewhere in the dark cold water, and for some reason known only to God, it had fired a missile at them. "Red alert! All hands to battle stations! Activate electronic countermeasures, now! All weapon systems on-line!"

"Captain! We are being illuminated! The radar has locked on to us!"

Alarms rang throughout the ship. The hull of the small ship resounded with the booted feet of running men.

"Man the anti-aircraft guns! Prepare for incoming missile! It will be skimming the surface and coming in low and fast!"

"Captain! I'm tracking an object. It isn't following a sea-skimming profile, it is—" The electronics officer shook his head in wonder. "Captain, the object is above us!"

"Above us?" Vital blinked. "That's impossible. What altitude?"

"Just above one hundred thousand feet. Captain, I read its attack angle at over eighty-degrees, speed…Mach 6!"

Vital was appalled. There was no way a missile could be coming down at them at a nearly ninety-degree angle. "Lieutenant, that would mean the object is coming from outside the atmosphere."

"I would have to agree with you, sir."

"Check your systems."

The lieutenant quickly tapped keys. His face twisted into a frown. "I show all systems functioning perfectly." His face twisted into an even deeper frown. "Captain, the object is decelerating rapidly. I read it at Mach 5…Mach 4…Mach 3…"

"It's braking?" The captain leaned over his officer's shoulder and stared at the screen. Air friction would slow an object, but to slow that quickly implied drag chutes or retro-rockets. "Lieutenant, I believe we're observing some kind of reentry from space."

The lieutenant nodded. "So it seems. It's definitely braking. Captain, do you think it's some kind of satellite?"

Vital nodded. "I can think of no other explanation." He scratched his jaw. "What is its current radar activity?"

"It's continuing to illuminate us, Captain." He tapped the keys of his computer. "Our computer library has no record of this radar signature. It's completely anomalous. It's still heading toward us."

Captain Vital shook his head. It didn't surprise him that they couldn't recognize the radar signature. The Russians and the Americans had all sorts of strange things in orbit they didn't bother telling the captain of the *Prat* about.

"Should we stand down from red alert?"

"No," the captain answered as he watched the screen. "All ahead full. Let's get out of its way. Prep the skiff and break out marking buoys. If it looks safe, I want to attempt a salvage when it hits the water."

The hull vibrated as the engines went to full power. The *Capitan Prat* began to knife ahead through the dark water at emergency war power as it strove to reach its top speed of thirty-two knots. "What's the object's current speed?"

"Object's velocity has stabilized at a constant Mach 2.5, Captain."

That was still very fast. Too fast for a satellite that had deployed its chutes or was using rockets. Of course, the fact that it was reentering over Drake Passage implied that something might be wrong with it. If it didn't slow it was going to hit very hard.

"Speed still remains constant, Captain. Mach 2.5." The lieutenant suddenly looked up. "Do you think it could be some kind of shuttle or space plane?"

The idea was very intriguing. "I don't know, Lieutenant. It could—"

"Captain!" The young officer nearly leaped from his seat. "Object has changed flight angle. It is maneuvering to maintain a collision course. Its radar has gone into rapid-pulse mode. This is an attack profile."

Vital's head snapped to his weapons officer. "Do you have a lock on the object?"

"Yes, Captain! Fire control radar is tracking."

"Go active!"

The *Capitan Prat*'s 901 fire control radar was mounted almost directly over the bridge. It was tilted up at nearly ninety degrees as it monitored the object coming down at them. The weapons officer gave it the command to go active. The fire control radar shot out a tight radar beam that illuminated the incoming object like a flashlight and continued to point at it like an accusing finger.

"We have radar lock."

"Fire!"

On the stern of the ship the Sea Slug missile roared off its launch rail.

The Sea Slug was an old missile, initially deployed in 1962. It had undergone a series of upgrades through its service, but it was still obsolete by modern standards. The fact that it had to ride a radar guide beam rather than use an onboard guidance system of its own showed its age. However, it was still a very large and powerful missile, large enough to use against surface targets as well as hostile planes and missiles. It would ride its guide beam fearlessly against anything it was pointed at.

The weapons officer shouted in alarm. "Captain! Object is emitting electronic countermeasures! The guide beam is being broken! Missile has lost lock!" The weapons officer and the electronics warfare officer both looked close to panic. The air above the ship looked clear and calm to the naked eye. In the radar spectrum the world had gone insane. Their screens showed phantom images, and huge blots of white noise hissed from the speakers. Signals had been jammed.

The captain roared. "Prepare to fire Seacat!"

The Seacat was a much smaller and more modern missile. The weapons officer snarled in fear and frustration. "Their range is too short! The object's speed and attack angle are too great!''

"Fire anyway!"

"Object within range! Firing!"

The Seacat missile shrieked from its quad launcher.

"Captain, we can't get an attack profile on the object!"

"Go to guns!"

The twin 114 mm cannons mounted on the bow whirled on their turrets. The gaping cannon muzzles rose and then ground to a halt at the top of their arcs.

"Captain, we can't get elevation. The guns can't point high enough. The object is coming straight down on us!"

Out on the deck the staccato snarl of the 20 mm anti-aircraft guns ripped into life. The two guns were mounted on either side of the radar tower. Both were being manually aimed by able seamen. Both men were pointing their guns nearly straight up and the gunners squinted as they fired blindly at the object coming down on top of them.

Captain Vital slammed down his fist. "Put out a distress call! We are—''

The object slammed directly amidships on the *Capitan Prat*. The hull shuddered as the armored body of the object punched through the decks and then detonated deep within the ship. The spine of the destroyer shattered with the blow, but her death throes were far from over. The Sea Slug missile magazine ran eighty yards through the center of the ship with twin tubes each holding fifteen of the large missiles. The thirty missiles in the magazines went off like a chain of gigantic firecrackers as the unidentified object exploded and detonated their warheads. The thirty rocket motors of the missiles exploded and the interior decks were torn open and engulfed in a firestorm of burning rocket fuel. The destroyer also carried 38 French Exocet missiles. As fire swept through her magazines, the even bigger Exocet warheads began detonating.

For long moments the damaged destroyer roiled, weapons detonating orange flashes in the dark water, and then the last of the twisted wreckage of the *Capitan Prat* sank to the bottom of the Antarctic Ocean.

**14**

*Asunción, Paraguay*

Mack Bolan smiled at Jack Grimaldi. "So what's the news?"

"Well, Chile lost a destroyer late yesterday afternoon. Sank right to the bottom of Drake Passage."

"I hadn't heard that."

"Well, it's no wonder. I'd heard you've been busy. How have things been here in Paraguay?"

"Informative. Tell me more about this destroyer."

"The *Capitan Prat*. It was a former British air-defense missile destroyer, recently under Chilean colors. It was lost with all hands."

Bolan's instincts were prickling. "Well now, that's rather odd, don't you think?"

"It is. The initial explanation is that she got her belly ripped out by a submerged iceberg. Or she suffered some kind of internal fire."

"You'd think there would be survivors."

"Yeah. The news is saying that she was an old design and carried her AA missiles in twin magazines that ran horizontally through a good portion of the ship. If the rip caused internal fires, or if someone on board did something monumentally stupid, she would have gone off like a string of firecrackers. The Chileans removed the internal missile magazines from several other ships of the same design they bought from the British."

"Did she get out a distress call?"

"Nope."

Bolan shook his head. "I don't buy it."

Grimaldi grinned. "Neither does the Bear."

"What does he think?"

"He thinks someone took out the *Capitan Prat*."

"Does he have any idea who?"

Grimaldi shrugged. "Not a clue."

Bolan ran over the idea in his mind. Given the current international situation, there seemed to be no reason to sink a Chilean destroyer. He couldn't believe a British submarine captain would be so dumb as to mistake it for an Argentine ship, much less start a war over a single destroyer cruising in Antarctic waters. Argentina had been in conflict with Chile before, but the last thing she needed now was an international crisis on two fronts. It made no sense, but Bolan didn't believe in fully armed missile destroyers going missing without a trace.

"No one is going to check out the wreckage?"

"I doubt it. Chile doesn't have the deep-diving resources to send any submersibles to the bottom of Drake Passage, and I don't think she'll be willing to spend the money to do so. The destroyer was old and her fighting technology was obsolete by about two decades, even with her most recent refits. The Bear thinks they'll just chalk it up as a loss. I'd have to agree with him. There's really nothing that Chile can do to investigate the situation."

Bolan smiled coldly. "That's very convenient for somebody."

"You know, Argentina didn't do so well the last time they took on Britain, maybe they felt like they needed a little target practice before they got down to real business," Grimaldi suggested.

Bolan gave him a look. Grimaldi shrugged. "Okay, so it

wasn't that funny, but with everything else that is going on, it kind of makes you think.''

''Yeah, it does.''

''So, what's the plan?''

''You're going to get hold of a helicopter.''

''Okay. Then what?''

''We're going to go visit a guy named Nico Souza.''

*São Paulo, Brazil*

THE HUMIDITY was ninety percent, and the temperature matched it. Bolan looked at the old Huey helicopter. He had ridden in a thousand birds like her and had a great deal of faith in the design. Grimaldi frowned at it. He would have preferred something sexier. Bolan didn't want sexy. He wanted inconspicuous.

He turned to Schwarz. ''What have you got?''

''The CIA branch office here in Brazil has been watching Souza's residences. He's got a lot of them, and the people they could spare us are spread pretty thin. But they say most of his houses have suddenly been abandoned except for the live-in servants.''

''What about the address on the river we got from our buddy Simon?''

''They say there are lights and activity inside, but no one is coming in or out. Definitely armed guards on the premises.''

Bolan nodded. ''Looks like they've circled the wagons. That's where we hit them. What's the news from Buenos Aires?''

''Dr. Lopez says he's sure he's being followed.''

Bolan thought about Lopez. He was a brave man and he was sticking his neck way out. ''Is there anything we can do for him?''

Schwarz didn't look happy. The old medical examiner had

won his respect as well. "If he goes to the American or British Embassies, we can give him sanctuary there, but if he goes on helping us and stays on the street, he's a target. The CIA in Buenos Aires says they have orders not to have embassy personnel active on this one. Everyone has to be deniable. We can't give him any bodyguards. If he's in trouble, he can bolt for the embassy, but unless we're with him, he's on his own."

The Executioner let out a sigh. "What else?"

"Well, the boys you, Rafe and Lopez took down in the morgue are dead, killed in custody. Someone got to them."

Bolan had expected that, but not so fast. Executing the first batch in a hospital was one thing. Being able to reach out to federal detainees being arraigned for serious felonies was another. "Killed how?"

"Poison. It wasn't a subtle one either. According to Lopez, those boys died real quick and real ugly."

"Any lead on what kind of toxin it was?"

"The doctor did the autopsy himself. He says he has never seen that particular toxin before. He says it looks and behaves like some kind of botanical poison, something that occurs naturally."

Bolan's eyes narrowed. "Something tropical?"

Schwarz followed his friend's logic. "Yeah, he suspects something out of the rain forest. Something Brazilian."

"See if you can get blood samples flown to the Bear. I want the FBI forensics lab to do a full workup on it. Then I want the results run against botanical studies of the Amazon basin and ethnographic studies of the known Brazilian tribes. It's a long shot, but if we can find out where the poison came from and who uses it, it might generate a lead of some kind."

"You got it."

"Anything else?"

"Your girlfriend Cecilia is asking about you. You haven't dropped by the embassy. She's afraid you're dead. She's getting hysterical.'' Schwarz smiled coyly. ''I think she likes you.''

Bolan had bigger concerns at that moment. Encizo walked down the tarmac staggering under bags of gear. ''Are we a go?''

Bolan nodded. ''The target hasn't changed. We hit Souza's house on the river. We leave in one hour.''

''How do we play it?''

''We take the river in scuba gear. If we get in and keep things under control, we leave the same way and Jack picks us up with the boat two miles downriver. If things get hairy, Jack comes in and we extract by helicopter, ditch it someplace convenient, and then use the river again to make it to the safehouse.'' Turning to Encizo, he asked, ''You got the boat?''

''I've got it.''

''Let's roll.''

MACK BOLAN swam through the black water of the Tiete river, kicking his swim fins steadily. The river was large, deep and slow-moving, and they had inserted two miles upstream from their target so the current was with them and would be with them when they swam farther downstream for extraction. The swim was easy, but Bolan and his team were operating in almost total darkness. Nico Souza's house on the river was located near the edge of town. The light coming from other houses on the river and the small lamps hanging over the numerous wooden piers and boat docks only penetrated a few scant feet into the dark water and then was swallowed up by blackness.

Bolan looked down at his swim board. Its luminous gauges glowed dimly. He was seven yards below the surface and had gone nearly two miles since entering the water. The air in his regulator tasted tinny, but it always did. The soldier swam through the blackness. He turned his head and his fingers trailed across his swim board to the right-hand console. He flicked the first button twice. At the right edge of his swim board pinpoints of blue light pulsed. A moment later pricks of blue light flickered back. A moment later the answering light flashed again.

McCarter was in formation on Bolan's right, and Encizo was still on McCarter's wing. Blue-light lasers cut through dark water better than any other light in the spectrum. The laser signaling lights on the front and sides of the swim boards were very small and very powerful. However, being lasers, they were also very focused. In such dark water anyone more than a yard or two above them would be unlikely to notice anything. Bolan's team was maintaining the preset seven-yard depth and they were keeping formation. The soldier then clicked his left-hand lasers and Schwarz's own lights flickered back.

The water began to rumble and vibrate, and Bolan slowed his pace slightly. The vibration grew louder and he looked up into the vault of darkness above him. The drone of the motor grew in intensity and the blackness above roiled as a motorboat cut the surface above him. The motor's wash rolled over him and Bolan checked his depth and corrected his position. The blue-light lasers flickered in the gloom again. The team maintained depth and formation.

Bolan swam toward the target. His odometer indicated they should be near Souza's house. The soldier pulsed his lasers quickly in the prearranged signal. He was going up for a look. The Executioner rose through the murk. A few scattered orange and yellow lights began to glow on the surface above him like smeared stars, and he angled away from them toward the darker gloom on the west riverbank.

The top of Bolan's head and the top edge of his diving mask broke the surface of the Tiete. The western side of the river was little more than a grassy bank. Much of the Tiete was normally overhung by trees. It seemed Nico Souza didn't want a screen of vegetation where someone could observe him from across the river. Bolan scanned Souza's riverfront perimeter.

A pair of powerful-looking speedboats were docked beside each other at a good-sized wooden pier. Towering over them was a larger yacht. A small padlocked shed stood at one end of the pier, and next to it the pier had its own gas pump.

Bolan submerged and flicked his signal lights. Lasers cut through the blackness and signaled for the team to rise. Four heads barely broached the surface of the water. Bolan spoke very low. "Gadgets."

"Yeah?"

Bolan's eyes followed the sleek lines of the red and white powerboat that floated at the dock. "I like that boat on the right."

"You want me to wire it?"

"I do, and I want the boat next to it and the yacht scuttled on my say-so. Oh, and while you're at it, see about swimming under the gas pump and wiring it and the shed to blow as well."

"You've got it." Schwarz sank back into the blackness. Bolan scanned the house. The house sat on a small hill that rose up away from the river. The grounds formed a long, wide, uphill killing zone that Bolan didn't like at all.

McCarter could sense the big man's mood. "You don't like it."

"Nope."

"Neither do I. They may have had time to do some thinking since we hit Paraguay."

"It's time we had Mattos make a phone call."

Bolan, McCarter and Encizo swam slowly forward to the boats. Schwarz slid silently out of the water and rolled into the cockpit of the speedboat that Bolan had indicated. The Executioner and the rest of his team slid their swim boards into the boat and then pulled themselves up and hunkered down in the four-seat passenger area. Schwarz craned his head around. "I've got this baby wired and she has a full tank of gas. I put charges on both of the other boats and I wired the bottom of the shed and the gas pump as well."

Bolan shucked off his tank and pulled the plastic cover off his pack. He attached his radio to his web gear and pulled the water protector off his weapon. He checked the loads in the Colt submachine gun and the M-203 grenade launcher. Schwarz broke out the satellite link and opened the line to the Farm. Bolan spoke into his mike.

"Bear."

"Reading you loud and clear," Aaron Kurtzman answered.

"It's time to drop a person-to-person with Souza."

"The satellite is ready. You have about a forty-minute window."

Bolan patched in to Grimaldi. "You have our boy ready?"

"Mattos is here with me. We're ready to make the call."

"Do it."

Simon Mattos was in the back of the helicopter. Bolan listened as they dialed the contact number he had for Souza. Once again the signal was shot to the satellite and bounced down to commercial relays. The phone picked up on the first ring.

"Where the hell are you?"

Mattos's voice came across the line. "Here. In São Paulo."

"What the hell are you doing? Why did you leave Paraguay?"

"Someone shot up my men at the house."

"I had heard that. I also heard you were taken off by the police."

"By two detectives that I own. We didn't go to the police station. We switched vehicles and got out of town."

Bolan could imagine the wheels turning in the mind of the other party. Neither one was using names, they wouldn't be that stupid, but Bolan assumed that this was the voice of Nico

Souza, and with any luck, he was in the house across the river speaking with Mattos right now.

"Why did you wait so long to call?"

Mattos was working well with his script. "I think the American somehow broke into my phone line and traced me. I can think of no other way they could have found me. I was only a voice to Aigular and Salcido."

"That's true. So why are you endangering me now, idiot."

Mattos paused. "I'm calling from a pay phone. They can't have the entire Brazilian telephone exchange bugged."

"Ah." The voice considered for a moment. "Who are these two detectives who helped you?"

"Esposito and Esposito."

The voice grunted in grudging amusement. After the War of the Triple Alliance against Paraguay, less than thirty thousand adult males were left in the entire country. It was said a man could ride from *rancho* to *rancho* from dawn to dusk and find a dozen willing widows in each one. It was a running joke in South America that all Paraguayans were really named Esposito, and huge numbers of them were. "You'll wait while I have this checked out."

"Sure."

"Are you safe?"

"I believe so."

"Were you followed?"

"I don't see how. I rented a helicopter to get here."

"Very well. Call me from that same pay phone, at this number, in one hour."

"One hour. I understand."

The line clicked off.

"Bear, did we get that?"

"All we needed. Satellite triangulation says that the phone call originated about fifty-five yards due south from your position."

Bolan looked out across Nico Souza's vast backyard, which

faced the river. "All right. We're going in. Jack, get your bird airborne. We may need very fast extraction."

"What about Mattos?"

"Tell him to sit back and enjoy the ride. We may still need him."

"I'm taking her up. Grimaldi out."

Bolan kept his eyes on the house. "All right, let's move."

The four men slid silently out of the speedboat's cockpit and fanned out across the wide expanse of lawn. Bolan could see lights in the house but little sign of activity. He and his team dropped and hugged the ground as a man with an M-16 rifle walked around from the side of the house, but the lawn itself was in darkness. He peered out over them at the river and then resumed his walk around the house's perimeter. Bolan and his team rose and moved forward at a crouch. The Executioner stayed in shadow and avoided the puddle of light thrown out by a window as he approached the back patio.

The back door was a huge pane of sliding glass, with a screen door to let in the breeze from the river but to keep out insects. American country-western music came from the house, and the smell of breaded steak and frying plantains wafted onto the patio. Bolan loosened a pair of CS tear gas grenades on his belt. He would have preferred Adamsite for its instant incapacitation, but he'd had no time for some to be rushed to São Paulo. And CS was nasty enough, particularly indoors. Yet someone with the proper motivation could still squeeze a trigger after they were exposed to it.

Bolan whispered into his mike. "All right, McCarter and I go in the back. Rafe, Gadgets, find a way on the side."

"Roger." Encizo and Schwarz disappeared into the shrubbery that hugged the side of the house.

Bolan moved quickly to the screen door. It opened into a large room with sofas and an entertainment center, which took up an entire wall. No one was currently in the room, and the system was off. The music had to be coming from somewhere else. Bolan looked at the screen-door handle. It was a simple affair with a thumb lever that raised a hook into the jamb. The hook was down—unlocked. He slid open the door and quickly entered the room. McCarter came after him.

Encizo spoke in Bolan's ear. "We have a guard coming our way. Let him pass or take him out?"

"Take him."

A small hallway led off from the living room. Bolan could hear the music coming from the hall, along with the odor of food and the sound of women's voices.

Encizo spoke again. "We're in. Inside a bedroom. We have one guard down. We encountered one servant. She is secured."

Bolan crouched by the hall entry. "Can you get any information out of her?"

"I tried to ask her about Souza and she started yammering in some dialect I don't recognize."

Bolan frowned. He suspected that might become a theme. Brazil had a thousand languages, and other than the smattering of Portuguese that Encizo knew, the team didn't speak any of them. "Make sure she's secure and continue your sweep."

"Roger."

Bolan moved down the hall into the kitchen. Two women were cooking, chatting. One woman turned and her dark eyes grew huge as she stared at the muzzle of Bolan's weapon.

Bolan spoke quietly. "Where is Souza?"

The woman stared at him for a moment before her eyes were drawn back irresistibly to the suppressed submachine gun with the grenade launcher attached to it. The other woman nearly dropped her frying pan in horror. Bolan grimaced. "Souza. Nico Souza."

The women crouched back slightly. It was obvious they didn't understand a word he said. It was also obvious that they did not know who Nico Souza was. At least not by that name. Alarm bells began to sound in Bolan's mind.

"Jack."

Grimaldi's voice came over the noise of his helicopter. "What's happening?"

"Are you still connected to the Bear?"

"Affirmative."

"Make another phone call."

Bolan waited. Over his earpiece he heard the phone ring. A moment later it picked up. "What's happening?"

Simon Mattos spoke. "I think I've been followed."

The line was silent for a moment except for the noise of Grimaldi's rotors. "Simon, why are you in a helicopter?"

The phone went dead. The hairs were prickling on Bolan's arm. "Did we get that?"

"We did. Satellite triangulation says that you're right on top of the signal. Within ten yards. No mistake."

"Could Souza be somewhere else and we're just picking up some kind of relay from this site?"

"No way. The satellite's tracking the signal through the commercial relay. If it was being bounced from somewhere else, we'd know it."

The situation came to Bolan with icy clarity. "Rafe, Gadgets, David: Souza is here. He's right beneath us. He's bunkered in the basement. This is a trap."

"Roger, what do you want to do?"

"Jack, how close are you?"

"One minute."

"Give us a flyover. Use your night-vision equipment. Tell me what you see."

"Affirmative."

Bolan pointed at the floor, and the two women dropped to the tiles like stones. The Executioner crouched. The sound of a low-flying helicopter began to vibrate the windows. Rifle fire erupted outside.

"There are hostiles all around the house! Closing in, platoon strength! There are boats on the river, activity on the dock. I'm taking fire!"

"Break off and get out of range! Orbit until I tell you otherwise."

"Affirmative. Breaking off."

Windows began shattering as weapons were trained on the house. Bullets tore through the kitchen window and began ripping into the cupboards. Bolan flipped up the sight on his grenade launcher. "Gadgets, blow the yacht and the gas pump!"

"Affirmative!"

The house shook. The night outside the kitchen window lit up in lurid orange. Fire shot into the sky in a column of burning gasoline pushed by high explosives. Shouts and screams came from the backyard.

"Rafe, find Souza's bolt-hole. Try the master bedroom."

"I'm on it!"

Bolan rose and fired his grenade launcher. The frag grenade sailed out the shattered kitchen window and detonated on the lawn. McCarter's launcher boomed down the hall and a grenade sailed out the screen door. The grenade went off with a crack, and men screamed as metal fragments buzz-sawed through the air in a lethal fifteen-yard sphere of destruction.

A dim boom went off in the front of the house. Encizo's voice came over the radio. "They're all over the place!"

"Masks on!"

The two women on the floor screamed as more bullets struck the house. Bolan pointed at the pantry door. "Move!"

It didn't require a grasp of English. The two women crawled across the kitchen floor and piled into the pantry. The door slammed behind them.

"All right, gas the place!"

Bolan pulled on his mask and sealed it around his face. He took the two CS tear gas canisters from his belt and pulled the pins. He dropped one to the kitchen floor and the gray smokelike gas began to pour across the kitchen floor. He tossed the second one past the kitchen into the dining room beyond. Tear gas began to pour in from the hall where McCarter was.

The gas would linger for ten to fifteen minutes, enough to give them the edge if the house was stormed, but it was a temporary measure at best. The old Huey Grimaldi was flying was no armored gunship. If four-dozen men opened on him with automatic rifles as he tried to land for an extraction he would never take off again. They needed a way out fast.

"Gadgets, what have you got?"

"I've got a steel door behind the master bedroom's closet."

"Can you open it?"

"It's a thick one. It'll take a few minutes."

Bolan quickly scanned the back patio and the lawn beyond. Clouds of gray tear gas roiled out of the broken windows and into the night. The gas was dispersing too fast. Rifle fire continued to hit the house in ragged hailstorms. Bolan racked open the breech of his M-203. "Rafe, David, Willie-Pete the perimeter."

"Affirmative."

Bolan slid a grenade into his M-203 and fired out the window. McCarter's and Encizo's weapons boomed seconds later. The orange glow of the burning dock outside was eclipsed by the incandescent yellow dazzle of burning phosphorus. Burning metal shot into the sky on streamers of superheated gas. White-hot smoke billowed outward from the detonation points and mixed with the tear gas that crawled from the house.

"McCarter, let's move!"

Bolan swept through the house. Bullets still flew through the open windows and hammered the walls outside but the white-phosphorus grenades had dissuaded them slightly. The searing gas was still thick in the hallways. Bolan came to an open door and found Schwarz standing in front of a closet in the master bedroom. Schwarz had taped a flexible shaped charge in a square around the steel doorjamb.

"Is it ready?"

The explosives expert nodded. "It took over half of what I had, but it should be enough."

All four men looked up as the house shook with the thunder of something detonating. McCarter shook his head. "That was a rifle grenade." A second detonation lit the hallway outside the room in orange fire.

Bolan jerked his head at the steel door. "Blow it."

The four men stepped back. Yellow fire shrieked around the jamb of the steel door. The door shuddered with a hissing crack as the shaped charge cut through the circumference of the door like a knife of molten metal and superheated gas. Bolan put his boot to the door and leaped aside. Encizo tossed a frag through as the metal door sagged inward and fell. The fragmentation grenade detonated with a crack. Bolan went through the door. A steep, narrow staircase of poured concrete led downward to another steel door.

"Blow it."

Schwarz began taping flexible shaped charge around the edges of the door with Encizo's help.

McCarter spoke from the top of the staircase. "Striker, they're in the house."

Bolan calculated the odds. "Use white-phosphorus if you have to, but keep them out of here."

"You've got it."

Schwarz stepped away from his work. "Ready."

"Do it."

He pressed the button on his detonator box. The flexible charge blew. Both Bolan and Encizo fired bursts past the fallen door, then stepped back as Schwarz tossed in a frag.

The grenade burst with a crack and sent lethal steel splinters scything through the room.

Bolan went through the door. The bunker was well appointed with a bed, a chemical toilet, a refrigerator and a small entertainment center. In one corner was a small desk with a computer. Fragments from the grenade had shattered the computer's monitor and torn up the stereo and television. On the opposite side of the room was another door.

Bolan moved into the room. Encizo ran a quick sweep of the contents while Bolan and Schwarz peered at the door. "What do you think?"

"I think it leads to the river. This is more than just a bunker, it's a bolt-hole."

"Can you do the door?"

Schwarz shook his head. "I can't blow it. I'm out of flexible charge." He examined the lock. "The lock is electronic. Maybe I can override it."

"Make it fast. David, what have you got?"

"I'm almost out of gas. No one without a mask is going to come into the master bedroom. If they're smart they're opening every window and door in the house. I'd say you've got ten minutes."

Bolan ran his eye over the massive door again. "Can you do it?"

"Striker, it's rigged to blow from the other side."

"Can you defuse it?"

Schwarz chewed his lip. "Maybe, if we had half an hour and full bomb-disposal equipment, but we don't have either one."

All three of them turned as the phone on the desk rang. Schwarz shrugged. Bolan went over and picked up the phone. "I'm kind of busy, Souza. What can I do for you."

The voice that had spoken with Mattos came across the line in clear, Portuguese-accented English. "I see you haven't blown yourselves up yet."

"Not yet."

"Why don't you put down your guns and come out?"

"I don't think so."

"Listen, I won't kid you. It won't be pleasant, but I know someone who wants to have a talk with you. It will hurt. It will hurt a great deal. My friend will want to make sure you hold nothing back during your conversation, but, it is likely you'll walk away with the full use of your limbs."

"Now, why would your friend want to do something like that?"

"It would amuse him to totally compromise American government operatives and then give them back when he was through with them."

"What kind of guarantee can you offer?"

Souza's voice grew jovial. "None whatsoever. But I've got a couple of RPG-7 rocket launchers and I'm thinking of having my men start shooting them down into the bunker once the smoke clears."

"Give me five minutes to talk it over with my men."

"I'll give you one."

Bolan hung up the phone. "Rafe, pull the refrigerator! Gadgets, grab the bed!"

Encizo heaved the refrigerator away from the wall and toppled it on its side. Schwarz heaved the mattresses off the bed's frame and pushed it over as well. The two of them pushed the refrigerator to the stairwell and laid the bed's frame over it. Schwarz grabbed the mattresses and piled them behind the refrigerator. Bolan hoisted the steel security door and laid it across the top of the bed's frame.

"McCarter! Willie-Pete the bedroom and bring the steel door from the stairs!"

"Roger that!"

Yellow-white light pulsed down from the top of the landing as the white-phosphorus grenade detonated in the bedroom. The whole house would be burning out of control within minutes. They had no way to go but forward. Schwarz looked at Bolan's bomb shelter. A refrigerator and double mattresses stood between them and the charge behind the door. With the steel security door laid on top of the bed's frame it looked like a fort a kid might make.

McCarter staggered down the stairs with the second steel door. He raised an eyebrow at Bolan's construction. He shook his head. "I see your Boy Scout days are coming back to you."

"Put it between the refrigerator and the mattresses. I want something solid between us and anything that comes flying along with the blast." He looked at Schwarz. He was one of the best demolition men Bolan had ever met. "Will it do?"

Schwarz looked at Bolan's bomb shelter critically. "Depends. I doubt Souza would use enough explosives to bring down his whole house. But I'm willing to bet that door is going to come off its hinges at very high velocity and bring a lot of concrete with it. The concussion will be horrendous, but with the stairwell open a lot of it should wash over us and funnel up into the house." He looked at Bolan quizzically. "Which one of us is going to be dumb enough to tamper with the door and set it off."

"I am."

Schwarz looked at Bolan and spoke dryly. "I suppose you have a plan for surviving that maneuver?"

Bolan pulled out an armor-piercing grenade from his bandolier and loaded it into his M-203. "I was thinking of using this."

Schwarz nodded. "That should do."

"All right, everyone get into the shelter. When the door blows, we should have a few seconds during which they think we're dead or incapacitated. Assuming we aren't, I want to be down the tunnel and hit them before they know what's happened."

Schwarz, Encizo and McCarter crawled under the steel

door and disappeared. Bolan crouched and aimed his weapon at the door's lock. He took a deep breath and exhaled.

Bolan fired.

He threw himself down and hands seized his web gear and yanked him beneath the shadow of the steel door. The grenade penetrated the door and detonated with a boom. Then hell erupted in the bunker. Bolan's eyes were squeezed shut but orange light lit his eyelids so that the veins pulsed across his vision. The floor shuddered and a thunderclap shook the house to its foundation. A great hand seemed to swat the refrigerator and the steel door. The men behind it were shoved three feet backward. The steel door above them was yanked up and smashed against the stairwell behind them. Dust and concrete rained down from the ceiling and blinding orange pulses were followed by blackness.

Bolan opened his eyes and shook his head. Other than a deafening ringing in his ears he could hear nothing. He yawned deeply several times and rose shakily to his feet. He pulled the mini-maglight from his web gear and switched it on. The great steel door lay on its side by the wall where the bed had stood. A good piece of the door frame had come away with it and chunks of concrete lay all around.

Schwarz, Encizo and McCarter rose by his side and flicked on their own flashlights. Encizo's lips moved but Bolan couldn't hear a word he said. The darkness and the deafness were disorienting and the Executioner found he had a hard time keeping his balance just standing. Schwarz suddenly sat hard and it took both Encizo and McCarter to stand him again. Bolan flashed his light in Schwarz's eyes and checked his pupils. They were both the same size. The explosives expert squinted his eyes shut and gave Bolan the finger.

The Executioner clipped his flashlight to the mounting bracket on the barrel-sleeve of his weapon. He jerked his head toward the gaping black hole where the door used to be. The four of them staggered down the narrow tunnel.

Bolan could feel the concrete beneath his feet sloping slightly downward. Ahead was another steel door. It was smaller than the first and circular. It had a big wheel in the middle and looked like a submarine hatch. They came to the door and Schwarz and Encizo scrutinized it. Schwarz shrugged his shoulders. Apparently he couldn't detect a trap.

Bolan looked at the door. Souza and his men had to be looking at it, and any second they would open it themselves to come and examine the carnage. They needed a distraction. Bolan yawned again to try and bring back some hearing. The ringing in his ears was a loud and constant whine. He took Schwarz by the shoulders and exaggerated his words with his lips.

"Blow the boats!"

Schwarz nodded and pulled out his remote detonator. Bolan, McCarter and Encizo shouldered their weapons. Schwarz punched a button. From where they were in the tunnel they could detect nothing. With luck the yacht on the dock had just gone up in flames. Schwarz pushed a second button that would blow up the second speedboat. Bolan nodded and McCarter took the big door's wheel and spun it. The massive steel bolts withdrew smoothly. Bolan, McCarter and Encizo put their boots to the door at the same time.

The steel door flew open on its massive hinges and stopped as it slammed into a man with a rifle. Bolan tossed a frag grenade and McCarter threw a flash-stun. Encizo seized the wheel and pulled the door shut after the grenades. The heavy steel door vibrated under his fingers slightly as steel fragments impacted against it. Bolan and McCarter put their boots to the door again and it swung open unimpeded.

Men lay on the ground, others staggered about with their weapons in their hands. Lethal fragments, the glare of burning magnesium and stunning concussive force had wrought havoc. Bolan slid past the door with his weapon firing in 3-round bursts. His team followed him. Outnumbered as they were, this was no place for mercy. Everyone with an AK-47 went down. Schwarz jerked Bolan's sleeve and pointed to a man lying off to one side.

He had a phone in his hand.

Bolan quickly checked him out. He matched Nico Souza's description. He was unconscious and had a nasty wound on his forehead but his skull appeared to be intact. He had been outside the frag's sphere of lethality.

Bolan looked at Schwarz, who, in turn, read his thoughts and nodded. He reached into his bag and pulled out an object the size and shape of a flattened medicinal gel-cap. He quickly checked the phone Souza carried and began pulling it apart.

McCarter jerked Bolan's shoulder and pointed. Men were coming from the house. The tunnel had led to the facade of a closed-off sewer pipe about forty yards from a strip of sand by the river. Bolan fired his M-203 and McCarter and Encizo followed with theirs. Bolan was pleased to notice he could actually hear the hollow booms.

The running men twisted and fell to the ground. The rest dropped and began firing back. Bolan and his team fell back out of the line of sight.

The Executioner looked to Schwarz. He nodded and held up the reassembled phone. He took a second device and slid it into Souza's wallet beneath his driver's license. Bolan loaded a personal defensive munition into his grenade launcher and jerked his head toward the river.

The team slid into the black water. Bolan grabbed his Beretta out of its holster before shrugging off his grenade bandolier and letting it sink. It was a sixty-yard swim to the dock. Ordinarily that would have been no problem except none of the team had swim fins or their swim boards and all of them were trying to swim with a submachine gun and a grenade launcher. It was also quite possible that they all had concussions. The water was black, but with the detonation of the gas pump and two of the three boats, the eerie red glow in the water led them straight to it.

Bolan's lungs burned and his temples pounded as if nails were being driven into them. He swam on and the roseate glow turned orange as it lit the pilings of the dock. The yacht was broken in half and had sunk into the mud. The second speedboat was too buoyant to sink but it was burning like a torch above them. Bolan kicked over to the third boat. He slid out of the water and grasped its rail.

Gasoline from the exploded gas pump had fountained across the dock and the speedboat was on fire. The cockpit looked all right. All the equipment they had left was still there. Two men with rifles stood away from the dock and peered downriver where guns were still going off.

Bolan slapped his M-203 over the rail and squeezed the trigger. The personal defensive munition was little more than a giant 40 mm shotgun shell. The swarm of buckshot tore out of the muzzle and cut down the two men in its lethal pattern.

Encizo came up over the rail and fired his grenade launcher at a cluster of men on the lawn. McCarter pulled himself half out of the water. He was dragging Schwarz. Bolan grabbed Schwarz by his web gear and pulled him out of the water. He was unconscious and blood was leaking from his nose. Bolan turned to Encizo.

"Get us out of here!"

The giant engine of the speedboat screamed to life with a roar. Smoke shot out its exhaust. McCarter rolled aboard and cast off the burning rope. Rifles began firing at their position. The fire burning on the dock made them an easy target.

Encizo threw the throttle full forward and the engine revved. Bolan and McCarter lost balance and fell to the floor of the cockpit as the boat shot forward. The burning gasoline on the boat's prow whipped backward in the wind and flared against the windscreen. Encizo jerked his head back as the flames tried to singe his wet hair.

Bolan pulled himself to a sitting position and grabbed a gear bag. The boat was shuddering from more than just the motor and Bolan knew they had taken hits. He pulled out a spare radio and punched in the frequency. "Jack, we need immediate extraction! I can't hear anything. Gadgets is hurt, I don't know how bad. We're in a speedboat heading down-river toward town. The boat has been hit! We're on fire!"

Bolan clicked off the radio and looked at Schwarz. Mc-Carter was trying to give him CPR in the rocking boat. Bolan slapped him on the shoulder and took his place while Mc-Carter put his hands on Schwarz's chest.

Bolan jerked back as river water came up with the first shove. Schwarz's body shook with a strangled cough and he weakly turned his head. McCarter grabbed Bolan and shouted in his ear. His voice sounded like it was coming from the bottom of a well.

"He passed out under the water!"

Bolan nodded. The boat suddenly slowed to a near stop. The soldier looked up and saw a helicopter hovering over the river before them. The chopper inched forward until its landing skid was nearly dipping into the boat's cockpit. Bolan and McCarter each grabbed Schwarz by his belt and man-handled him up while they clambered into the chopper. Encizo grabbed the skid and vaulted in. Grimaldi gave a look back to see that everyone was in and then the Huey shuddered as he shoved the throttle forward. The helicopter whirled on its axis and then dipped its nose as it shot down the river barely ten feet over the water.

Bolan glanced around the helicopter's cabin. It had taken rifle fire when Grimaldi had done his flyby. Mattos lay dead in the back in a drying pool of his blood. He had taken a burst from one of Souza's men on the ground.

Bolan's stomach lurched as the helicopter suddenly clawed for altitude. Grimaldi was heading for the mountains.

## 15

*Buenos Aires, Argentina*

Dr. Lopez peered narrowly into Schwarz's eyes and then turned to Bolan. "I suspect he has a moderate concussion."

The trip back to the safehouse had been torturous but uneventful. The CIA office in Brazil could do little to provide operatives or backup, but it could call in favors. Grimaldi had been given the coordinates to a privately owned airfield outside the city. A private plane had been waiting for them, fueled and with an approved itinerary into Buenos Aires. It had been a long and bumpy ride and Schwarz and the rest of them had suffered through it with bruised bodies and ringing ears. They had ditched all but their handguns on the plane and pulled on fresh clothes at the airport. From there they had switched one cab for another and then switched again. Bolan and his team had been barely able to crawl up the steps to the safehouse when they arrived in the dead of night. The team was exhausted. They had fought three battles in as many days. If the enemy found them there and hit them, they were finished. Bolan had been sorely tempted to seek the fortress-like safety of the American Embassy, but he knew the enemy's eyes were on it.

Being able to appear and disappear at will was just about the only advantage they had at the moment. Even though the embassy could give them rest, security and real medical attention, he couldn't let the enemy get a fix on them, no matter how battered and tired his team was.

Schwarz sagged back on the couch as Dr. Lopez stood back. "I'm fine."

The doctor looked at the explosives ace measuringly. "You seem all right, you have no amnesia and your eyes don't wander. You have severe ringing in the ears, which is a symptom of moderate to severe concussion, but then again, I'm informed you were in the middle of an explosion, so it could be an unrelated aural trauma. Without going to a hospital, there is no way to tell if there is swelling or bleeding in the brain. I recommend you take ibuprofen. A lot of it. If there is swelling or bleeding we need it to recede as quickly as possible."

Schwarz's eyelids visibly drooped. "Eight hundred milligrams every four hours, I promise, and I'll see a doctor at the first opportunity. You have my word on it." Schwarz closed his eyes wearily. Encizo began rummaging through the medical bag.

Bolan looked down at his friend and then at the doctor. He had seen more battle damage on more friends than he liked to think about. Head injuries were always the most anxious. The human brain was an uncertain thing. "You think it's okay for him to sleep?"

"It's probably the best thing for him." Lopez looked at Bolan meaningfully. "For you, too."

The Executioner had ignored the pain and exhaustion and forced himself to see his team to safety. Now it washed over him in a sickly wave. His limbs felt full of sand and his joints were rubber. "Akira?"

Tokaido looked up from his computer and pulled off his headphones. "What's up?"

"We're done in. Tomorrow we go to work on the tracers we left on Souza. We may be heading right back to São

Paulo, but right now need eight hours downtime. You think you can keep watch?''

Tokaido looked about at the filthy, battered, red-eyed warriors. ''Yeah, sure thing. No problem.''

Bolan took a deep breath. ''Thank you for coming, Dr. Lopez. Is there anything we can do for you?''

''Call me Tito.''

Bolan smiled tiredly. ''Anything you need, Tito?''

The doctor shrugged. ''My friends on the police force arranged for a diversion for me to get away and come here. I know that at home and at work I'm being watched by the enemy. I rather enjoy the feeling of being out of sight for the moment. I feel as if I can breathe. Perhaps I'll stay here and stand watch with your young friend here if you don't mind.''

''Not at all.''

Lopez looked around at the submachine guns and grenade launchers in the room. ''Have you a pump shotgun I might borrow?''

Bolan smiled. ''We must have one around here somewhere.''

*Deception Island*

WALDEMAR SALOME was appalled. ''How has this happened?''

Ladislao Dirazar had no good answer. ''I don't know. The Americans found Nico. They walked right into Souza's trap and they fought their way out of it. We lost most of our local muscle. There were huge fires and explosions. They lit up the river. Hundreds of people heard the firefight. Nico's house burned to the ground. The police are crawling all over the place. Too many to hush or buy off. I tell you, it's a disaster area.''

''Nico is dead?''

''No, he's alive.''

"Really?" Salome frowned as he looked out of the control bunker across the barren landscape of the Antarctic. "We thought Aigular was alive and it was really the American. We thought Ramon was all right but the American had compromised him. Now the American has hit Nico and you say he is alive and has escaped?"

"Not all of the men were killed. The Americans themselves were focused on escaping the trap. Nico was outside the tunnel when one of the Americans threw a grenade. I'm not surprised they didn't recognize him. Nico didn't look like himself. He looked like someone who had been beaten to death with a meat cleaver. He took a very bad wound to the head. Some of his men found him among the bodies and carried him to safety."

"Where is he now?"

"In a house we own, outside of São Paulo. They wanted to take him up the mountain to your mansion but the way the Americans have been following our trail I didn't think that was a good idea."

"You were right."

"He's surrounded by trusted men. He has received medical attention and I spoke with Nico myself. He sounded all right."

Salome rubbed his temples. He looked out at the massive shapes that dominated the island three hundred yards away. "Tell me, what is the news of the world?"

Dirazar's voice brightened. "You haven't heard?"

"We have CNN here, but I wish to know what you have heard on the continent."

"Our contacts in Chile say the *Capitan Prat* never even got out a distress call. She sank like a stone to the bottom of Drake Passage. They have no submersibles to go and investigate. The loss of the ship itself was barely a footnote in the news. No one suspects anything. It's already forgotten. I would describe the test run as an unmitigated success."

Salome allowed himself a small smile. "What's happening in the islands?"

"No change. The British had three ships stationed in the area before the crisis. The guided missile destroyer, *Manchester*, the antisubmarine warfare frigate, *Boxer*, and the frigate *Battle-axe* is in command, piloted by a Captain Nigel Harret. Our agents say he has a very good reputation and is very capable. The three ships are patrolling for Argentine submarines on the western side of the Falkland Islands, waiting to join the British task force when it arrives. We can't confirm it, but our contacts suspect that there is at least one, if not two, nuclear-powered hunter-killer submarines patrolling with them."

"Very well. We'll begin as soon as possible."

Dirazar's voice grew cautious. "The British ships are much more modern than the *Capitan Prat*. Their radar and defensive systems are much more sophisticated."

Salome shrugged as he scanned the deserted beach. A few shell-shocked penguins waddled about their nesting site. "The technicians assure me that it would take an American battleship or aircraft carrier battle group to pose a serious problem. Speaking of carriers, what have you heard about the British task force?"

"They're steaming at full power. They are expected to arrive in approximately two and a half weeks."

"Get me the approximate coordinates of the British ships *Boxer*, *Manchester* and *Battle-axe*. It is time to begin the second phase."

"Immediately. Also, I have spoken with the general as you have asked. He has chosen two targets that he believes will do."

Salome smiled like a wolf. The general was a fool, but he craved power. "Excellent. Give me the coordinates as soon as possible. What of the American?"

"We're watching both the British and American Embassies

in Argentina, Brazil, Uruguay and Paraguay. We don't believe he has entered any of them. He hasn't resurfaced since he escaped Nico's house.''

''Very well. I'm returning tomorrow. I wish the coordinates of both target areas ready for launch tonight. Contact me immediately when you have them.''

''Right away.''

The line clicked and Waldemar Salome looked out once more upon the tools of destiny. After this night, there would be no turning back for anyone involved. There would be a war, and nothing the diplomats, the United Nations or the American himself could do would stop the bloodshed.

*South Atlantic Ocean*

''THE *MANCHESTER* is burning, sir, she's sinking!''

Captain Nigel Harret looked out across the dark water. Orange fire and the yellow flashes of secondary explosions lit up the night. Black smoke obscured the stars. Her Majesty's royal guided missile destroyer *Manchester* was sinking beneath the waves of the South Atlantic. She was the air-defence ship of the tiny British force that was holding position off the Falkland Islands until the main task force arrived. She had powerful early warning and detection radars and the weapons to deal with incoming aircraft and antiship missiles. There had been no warning, no known hostile ships anywhere within range. No Argentine aircraft could get out this far without tanker refueling. British Intelligence said none had been spotted taking off from mainland Argentina. Off to port, the last of Her Majesty's frigate *Boxer* was also sinking into the depths.

Harret grimaced. There could be no doubt. The Argentines had to have a sub out there. Probably more than one.

''Get me the *Triumph* on the horn! Now!''

Captain Harret stood on the bridge of HMS *Battle-axe*. The

antisubmarine warfare frigate's sonar was actively pinging for a target. Immense pulses of sound thundered beneath the surface of the ocean and spread out in all directions. None of the pulses came back, save one, and that was one of their own. Her sonar phone called out through the water to Her Royal Majesty's nuclear hunter-killer submarine *Triumph*. The sound waves tore through the water for the sonar of the submarine to pick up.

"Captain, I have the *Triumph*. She's actively pinging. She says they can find no targets. Repeat, she can find no targets."

Harret's fists clenched. "Goddamn it, Lieutenant! There has to be something out there!"

"*Triumph* says she has no targets, sir."

*Battle-axe*'s own sonar operator confirmed the sub's assessment. "Sir, we have nothing. Just *Triumph*. *Boxer* and *Manchester* are going down."

Harret swore. The Argentine submarine force was old. He wasn't going to sell them short, even old diesel-electric submarines had the ability to lurk quietly. But two of Her Royal Majesty's best surface combatants were sinking beneath the waves. Their passive sonars should have heard the Argentine's launch. Their radars should have detected the missiles skimming the surface. If it had been aircraft, *Manchester* should have detected both the aircraft and the missiles they had launched.

"Captain," the radar operator shouted. "We have another object, coming down at a ninety-degree angle. Mach 6! Heading on collision course! We're being illuminated!"

*Battle-axe* was already using her full suite of electronic warfare countermeasures.

"Full speed ahead! Emergency war power! Launch Sea Wolf!"

The six-cell launch boxes on *Battle-axe*'s decks snapped open. Fire erupted from the steel launchers and squat cruciform wing missiles screamed out over the prow and began to climb rapidly.

"Sea Wolf One and Two, launched! We have lock on unidentified object. It has decelerated to Mach 3. Object is altering course to follow us. Collision course being maintained. Captain, object is jamming us! We're losing our lock on it! Sea Wolf One has lost radar lock!"

"Go to optical. Use infrared to guide her in."

The weapons officer swept the sky with his infrared optical sight. "Captain! I can't see the object on infrared."

"Captain, Sea Wolf Two has lost radar lock. Object's radar has gone to fast pulse attack mode."

Captain Harret's mind was very clear. He didn't know exactly what was happening, but he understood the situation well enough. Whatever was attacking them was a ship killer, and one nothing in the British fleet had any defence against.

"Lieutenant, get a message to the fleet. Tell them the situation."

"Captain, communications are being jammed across all frequencies."

"That's impossible! A missile can't have that much—" Harret stopped. His mind made an intuitive leap and he saw what might possibly be happening. It staggered his mind.

"Captain! Object closing!"

"Get on the phone to *Triumph*! Tell her that—"

Her Royal Majesty's antisubmarine warfare frigate *Battle-axe* groaned as she was struck. Her upper decks were penetrated and then the high explosive warhead detonated deep within her bowels. Her stores of Sea Wolf and Exocet missiles began exploding and her main fuel cells ignited even as the primary detonation broke her spine. *Battle-axe* was gutted and breaking apart as she burned out of control.

Four hundred feet below the surface, HMS *Triumph* sat under the thermocline layer. She had ceased active pinging. Unless some other source of sonar went active to find her, she was invisible. She made no noise, but she listened very intently.

The sea was full of noise.

HMS *Boxer* and *Manchester* still groaned as they sank. Bulkheads burst and caved in and the torn girders of the superstructures howled in agony as they twisted into the depths. Vast pockets of displaced air belched and bubbled to the surface. *Triumph* had listened to three of Her Majesty's most modern surface combatants die in as many minutes.

Argentina had just declared war.

The *Triumph*'s captain stood white-knuckled and seethed. Except for *Triumph* herself, the Falkland Islands were now defenceless. The attack center of the sub was deathly quiet. The explosions of the dying vessels could be dimly heard vibrating through her hull.

"Captain, shall we take her to antennae depth?"

Captain James Smith let out a long, slow breath and nodded at his commanding officer. "Yes."

The submarine slowly rose to one hundred feet and her antenna array pierced the waves of the surface. The captain looked at his communications officer. "Any radio traffic?"

"None, sir."

"Captain, do you wish to surface and search for survivors?"

Smith's jaw clenched. "No." He couldn't afford to. Three ships of Her Majesty's fleet were going down to their graves. *Triumph* had done a full passive sweep when the foreign objects had first been detected. She was one of the most modern nuclear hunter-killer submarines in the world. Only the very latest American designs could rival her capabilities.

There was no Argentine diesel boat out there. There was no hostile ship. The captain was willing to bet his life on it. *Boxer* had reported no antiship missiles, much less aircraft within range to launch them. It was as if the three ships had been struck down by thunderbolts from on high.

"Lieutenant, go to Code Red Six." The captain then turned to his communications officer. "Get me London."

**16**

*Buenos Aires, Argentina*

"Good God." McCarter's face was like stone as he gazed at the television screen.

The story made Bolan's blood run cold. He sipped his coffee as he took in the images of destruction. The scene looked like a smaller version of Pearl Harbor after the Japanese had attacked. The Argentine guided missile destroyer *Hercules* lay on its side burning out of control. The frigate *Espora* had burned to the waterline and was still slowly sinking. Rocket fuel and exploding missiles from the dying vessels had set fires and a whole section of the harbor was ablaze, including many smaller service ships and harbor vessels.

Bolan shook his head slowly. He looked over at McCarter. "I'd be curious to know how Britain did that."

McCarter continued to stare at the screen. "Striker, I really don't think we did."

"You don't think you could?"

"I'm not saying we couldn't. The U.K. has some capable submarines, better than the best Russian stuff and almost as good as the American models. It's possible one could have snuck in and torpedoed those ships, but once they did they would be spotted on sonar immediately. If it had approached to standoff range and fired cruise missiles, it would be the same situation. Argentine air defense has to be on alert. Britain could do the job, but it just couldn't get away clean. For that matter, if it was going on the attack, I believe I would have been notified and activated to go hostile behind enemy lines here in Buenos Aires."

McCarter's arguments matched Bolan's reasoning exactly. "I'd have to agree. I also believe if it had been your boys doing it, they would have made an all-out effort to sink the Argentine's one and only aircraft carrier." Bolan glanced at the television again. The aircraft carrier *Venti Cinco de Mayo* was visible beyond the burning ships, and she didn't have a scratch on her. "That also brings up the opposite question. How in God's name did Argentina manage to sink *Battle-axe*, *Boxer* and *Manchester* in a matter of minutes?"

McCarter took a deep breath. The sinking of three of his country's ships with the loss of all hands on board hadn't sat well with him at all. Bolan had never seen him so furious. However, the Phoenix Force leader's fury was as cold as ice. "I hate to say it, but I don't think they could have. The only way Argentina could have effectively engaged them would have been with her submarine fleet. If an Argentine sub had got within torpedo range and launched, the three ships would all have fired antisubmarine torpedoes back. Her helicopters would have launched and would have dropped depth charges. For that matter, I know personally that we had a nuclear sub with that group. If the Argentine subs had fired on our surface ships, she would have engaged them. I also know for a fact that she didn't. They all went down, and our sub didn't fire a shot. She never detected a thing."

"Then who could have done it?"

"The only people capable of doing it and getting away with it would be your government, Striker."

Bolan raised a surprised eyebrow. McCarter shrugged. It wasn't an accusation. "The only way I can possibly imagine doing it would be to attack at night using one of your B-2 stealth bombers armed with laser designated weapons. That could have done the trick rather nicely on both counts." He raised an eyebrow to match Bolan's. "Is there something you're not telling me?"

One corner of Bolan's mouth turned up slightly. It was a testament to the Briton's willpower that he could maintain a sense of humor at the moment. "I sure as hell hope not." Bolan rose from his chair. "I think I need to have a long talk with the Bear."

WALDEMAR SALOME grinned in savage triumph. He sat in the study of one of his houses in Ricoleta, one of Buenos Aires' wealthiest areas, the equivalent of Hollywood. Salome found the district offensive, but it was useful to him to have an apartment there. He held a copy of the *La Nacion*, the national newspaper of Argentina across his lap. There were only two things on the paper's front page. One was a damning aerial photograph of the Argentine ships *Hercules* and *Espora* lying in port, blackened and burning. The other was the headline. One word in massive black letters. *GUERRA!*

War. Salome leaned back in his chair and savored the sweet taste of victory in his mouth. It was war. A savage attack on the high seas against Britain, a slap in the face which couldn't be ignored and an attack on Argentine soil itself. There was nothing that the peacemakers could do. Both nations were boiling for vengeance. Both nations could protest they had done nothing, and neither side would believe the other, or bother to deny the attacks. It was far too late to stop the conflict. The newspapers of both nations screamed other words besides war. They screamed of death tolls, of resisting imperialism and fighting tyranny. They screamed of shed blood, sovereign soil and vengeance. England and Argentina had both declared war. The British fleet was already sailing and was little more than two weeks away. Argentina was marshaling her forces to meet it.

The world was indeed his circle now, his *roda*, and entire nations whirled in combat as he called the tune. Salome picked up his phone and punched a button. It answered on the first ring and Salome spoke. "Have you read the newspaper?"

"You have done it! You have really done it!" Nico Souza's voice was proof of his astonishment.

"You had doubts, then?"

"I never doubt anything you say you'll do, but you pay me to do your worrying for you."

"You worry like an old woman. I should double your pay."

Souza laughed. "So, it is truly a war. The general will be very pleased. He's looking forward to being the conquering hero."

"He's looking forward to being president, and as for being a conquering hero, we are handing him his victory over the British on a silver platter."

"Well, he'll enjoy the parade."

"He may enjoy anything he wants as long as he obeys. To be honest, I don't think he'll be president of Argentina for very long. He's an ambitious man. I believe he'll suffer a terrible mishap and someone more tractable will have to take his place."

"Well, my friend, you have done it. It's a complete success. Each test has been passed. Your idea has worked perfectly. It's war, and no one can stop it."

"Indeed, so far it has." Salome looked at the map on the wall and his eyes stayed on the South Atlantic and the tiny group of islands that England called the Falklands and Argentina the Islas Malvinas. Argentina was very likely to land an occupation force on the islands as quickly as it could. Even now, the British fleet was sailing under full steam toward the islands hell-bent on vengeance. The troop ships were loaded down in the water with SAS commandos, Royal Marines, the Queen's Life Guards, the Gurkhas and everything else they could muster. Britain's armed forces were small, but they were some of the most highly trained and motivated soldiers in the world. It was going to be a hell of a fight.

If Salome let it happen, which he had no intention of doing. The general was going to have his victory and ride at the head of a ticker-tape parade. England would be handed her worst defeat since Dunkirk.

Very soon it would be time to go to the next phase of the operation.

"BEAR, WE'RE STARTING to have something of a situation down here."

"Well you know, I believe you may be right." Aaron Kurtzman's voice sounded as if he was in the room with Bolan instead of a hemisphere away.

"What's happening on your end?"

Kurtzman sighed. "Well, Striker, it looks like we've got a war on our hands. The President is quietly asking all nations not to give aid or harbor to either side in an effort to contain the conflict. The United Nations is calling for a cease-fire and negotiations, but neither side is listening. Nationalism is running at fever pitch in both countries. Both sides are spoiling for a fight. It looks like they're going to get one."

"How do you see it?"

"Well, unless something freakish comes up that no one can predict, the conflict should remain a naval battle in the South Atlantic, with some infantry action on the Falkland Islands themselves. I can't imagine either side trying to actually invade the other's home country, the logistics are just too ugly. I suppose it would be possible for England to insert SAS teams to assassinate some people and blow up some facilities, but the distance from home is huge and the chance of successful extraction pretty grim. England has a few bombers that, with refueling, might be able to make it to Argentina, but their bomb load would be relatively minuscule, and Argentina will be watching for them. England does have a nuclear arsenal in her attack submarines, and they could certainly sneak close enough to use it, but there is no way in hell I can see England using thermonuclear weapons to settle this conflict."

"Neither can I."

"As for the Argentines, they just don't have the capability to reach out and touch the U.K. on their own soil. She could try to sneak in a couple of her own submarines and torpedo some ships in harbor, but I'm betting she's keeping every sub she's got close to meet the British fleet."

"I agree."

"I suppose there is a slim chance that the British might try to attack mainland Argentina again with conventional cruise missiles."

Bolan peered intently at the wall in front of him. "I don't believe they did the first time."

"I'm tempted to agree with you, except there simply is no other likely explanation. I've considered the possibility that the Russians did it, but why? What do they have to gain? I just don't see it. Whatever profit there might be, it would be inconsequential if it came out. They would be at war with England and Argentina, and even if no shot was fired back, the United Nations would condemn them, and nearly the entire western world would hit them with massive economic sanctions. The Russian economy is at rock bottom as it is. Sanctions would destroy it."

Bolan ran the framework of the situation out loud for the hundredth time. "So, some unknown third party."

"Almost impossible to believe, but go ahead, let's run through it again."

"Who stands to gain?"

Kurtzman considered. "Not England. They already own the Falklands. Losing ships doesn't profit them anything. I don't see their government toppling, win or lose."

"I agree. I think someone wants a war, and they want Argentina to win. But I don't think it's the Argentine government.''

"What facts do we have?"

"We have definite hostile activity in Argentina and Paraguay. It's connected, but we don't know how yet."

"Almost all the activity is criminal, Mack. Anyone with the right money could make players like that move. Even British Intelligence if they really wanted to."

Bolan conceded the point but his instincts told him he was still right. "The *Venti Cinco de Mayo* is still above water."

Bolan could hear Kurtzman shift in his wheelchair. "Well, you've got a point there. If the British military has even two brain cells to rub together, that would have been the primary target. Taking Argentina's only aircraft carrier is just about the best strategic move they can make given the nature of the conflict."

"So someone wants a war. They struck a heavy blow against England, but left Argentina with most of her capability intact. They want Argentina to win."

"What do they get out of it? If Argentina wins, the ruling government will be hailed victorious. They'll remain in power. Nothing changes hands other than the Falklands."

Bolan nodded. "What if the assassinations that kicked this whole thing off continue in Argentina. The Argentine president and his cabinet are then killed by supposed British SAS terror teams in revenge for losing the Falklands. What if certain generals, victorious generals, mind you, take over in this time of national emergency?"

Kurtzman was silent a moment. "Whoever put these generals back in power would be able to ask any price he wished."

"And if the oil fields north and south of the Falklands yield even half of what is expected, that price could end up in the millions."

"Try a billion over time."

"Bear?"

"What?"

"I want you to come up with a weapon, hypothetically."

"Shoot."

"You need to sink British ships in the South Atlantic. You need to overcome shipborne antimissile systems, armed with both surface-to-air missiles and automatic cannons when you get to within point-blank range. You need to overcome air-defence radar. You need to be invisible to infrared. You need to come in so fast and so quiet your targets have no time to react and you fear nothing that they might react with."

"That is a very interesting set of weapon parameters."

"Any ideas?"

Bolan could hear Kurtzman scratch his beard. "Well, off the top of my head, I'd try a B-2 stealth bomber attacking at night with laser-designated smart bombs. They would fall out of nowhere, come almost straight down. Most shipborne radars have a cone of blindness where something could sneak in if it was coming in almost vertically. They would come in ballistically, too. No rockets or jet engines to give an infrared imager something to find. That might just do the trick nicely."

"That's what McCarter came up with."

"David is a very intelligent man."

Bolan rolled his eyes. "Just for argument's sake, let's assume that the United States doesn't wish to instigate a war between England and Argentina, and that no B-2 stealth bombers or F-117 stealth fighters have currently been stolen from U.S. inventory."

"Well, now, that makes things a bit more difficult. It comes down to submarines again. Assume there is such a thing as a stealth sub no one can detect, and somehow Argentina, or someone who wants it to win back the Falklands, gets hold of one. It has to fire its weapons. It has to flood its torpedo tubes or launch its missiles. Torpedoes have to move with either screws or some kind of jet. Aerial weapons have to be propelled into the air somehow to reach their targets. Either way, no matter what you do, you announce yourself.''

''A stealth sub firing stealth torpedoes? Or stealth missiles?''

''Those are mighty big question marks, Striker. I won't rule them out. I know our research and development boys are working on such things, but you're assuming someone is using them now. Who built them? It's either us or the Russians. Maybe the Japanese, but I'm not buying it. Even granting you that, how does Argentina figure into it?''

Bolan frowned. Kurtzman was right. The situation just didn't compute. ''All right, let's assume it is technology you could use today. Available right here, right now. Off the shelf.''

Bolan could imagine Kurtzman shaking his head back in Virginia. ''Can't be done. I'm sorry.''

Bolan's eyebrows bunched in a frown. ''Bear, someone is doing it. Someone is doing it right now. I can feel it in my bones and I need you to tell me how.''

Kurtzman was silent.

''Bear, I need you to speculate. I don't care how crazy it gets, but give me something. Anything.''

Kurtzman was silent for long moments. He was a genius. He knew he was a genius. He was very unassuming about it. However, there was one thing he had learned to trust even more than his own staggering mental ability. That was the battle-earned instincts of Mack Bolan. He let out a very long sigh.

''All right. I'll come up with something, but we're speculating wildly here. Don't count on it being rational.''

''Power creates its own sense of rationality.''

''That's very true. Let me know if you come up with anything more I can work with.''

''Okay, let's change your parameters. We're assuming the

same weapon system hit the British ships off the Falklands and hit Argentina in Puerto Bel Grano."

"Okay."

"Let's assume the same weapon system took out the Chilean destroyer *Capitan Prat*."

"Well that gives us another coordinate to triangulate with, but why? It doesn't make any sense."

"Gadgets told me you thought someone took out the *Capitan Prat* deliberately."

"Well, that's what I suspect, but how does it compute into the current situation? I mean, think about it, why does someone want a war with Chile in all of this? Who stands to gain?"

"I agree with you. No one stands to gain. Given the current situation, the *Capitan Prat* has no strategic value. But Gadgets made a bad joke in São Paulo that stuck in my mind. He said the Argentines hadn't done so well in the last war, and maybe they needed some target practice."

Kurtzman's voice grew noticeably excited. "You think the sinking was a test run of our hypothetical weapon, don't you?"

"Well, think about it. A single Chilean destroyer with obsolete weapons and radar technology, operating alone in Drake Passage at the height of iceberg season. She was an easy target, far from home, and if all went well, neither Chile nor anyone else was going to go diving to investigate the wreckage. I couldn't pick a better target, could you?"

"No, I can't."

"Come up with something, Bear. Anything. Give me something to work with."

"I will. Like I said, it will be crazy, but I'm going to get the whole crew together, brew some coffee, and we're going to figure out a way to start a war between Argentina and England."

"Bear, if I was going to start a war, you'd be the first person I'd call."

"Well, I guess I'll take that as a compliment." Kurtzman's excitement over this exercise was tempered with concern. "What are you going to do in the meantime?"

"Well, we've got the CIA in São Paulo trying to see if they can detect the tracers we put on Nico Souza, but their range is limited. If Souza doesn't go back to downtown São Paulo it may be a wash. I think I may go to the American Embassy and see if I can pick up a tail."

"You're more likely to pick up a bullet in the head."

That was a highly likely prognosis. Bolan shrugged to himself. "Bear, I'm out of leads."

"Maybe you just want to go see your girlfriend."

Bolan paused. "You're talking about Cecilia?"

"Akira told me she was a babe."

"Akira spends too much time by himself."

"That's probably true."

A thought Bolan had filed away suddenly occurred to him. "Bear, what do you know about Brazilian martial arts?"

There was a moment of silence while Kurtzman mentally switched gears. "The national martial art of Brazil is *capoeira*. Why do you ask?"

"It was something I saw in Souza's house. There were a pair of African-looking musical instruments mounted on the wall along with a pair of machetes."

"That would be *capoeira*. When they practice they play African instruments. According to legend it was a martial art taken from West Africa and adapted by the slaves who were brought over to work the plantations in Brazil. It's very acrobatic and very lethal. Grimaldi is a savate man and he talks about *capoeira* men with awe. In the Brazilian barrios, if a fight was going to be to the death the fighters often fought with machetes in one or both hands and straight razors held in their toes while they did cartwheels and handstands. From what I know about it even casual practice is pretty spectacular to watch.''

Bolan nodded to himself. ''Find me everything you can about modern masters and their students. See if you can link Nico Souza to it. See if he belonged to any school or trained with any particular master. If Nico is high up in this thing, then maybe we can get a bead on who he is working with.''

''You know, your research parameters get more fascinating by the second.''

''I'll call you from the embassy.''

''Roger and out.''

Bolan leaned back in his chair. He knew that Kurtzman wouldn't sleep until he had solved the riddles he had been given. He suspected no one else on the Farm was going to sleep either. Battle fleets were sailing. Time was running out.

**17**

Mack Bolan drove through the gates of the American Embassy without incident. He wore a Threat Level III Kevlar body armor with ceramic trauma plate inserts beneath his coat, and the baseball cap he wore had thick Kevlar above the bill. Both the 9 mm Beretta 93-R machine pistol and the .44 Magnum Desert Eagle semiautomatic rode locked and loaded just beneath Bolan's coat.

No armed figures rushed between him and the embassy gates. No sniper's bullet spiderwebbed the windshield or shattered the windows of the rented Renault. He rolled into the embassy driveway. Three Marine Corps Embassy Guards scanned the street behind Bolan while the gates closed. The massive form of Corporal Samuels appeared at Bolan's window. Samuels grinned. He had enjoyed his stint as a secret agent in the subway station. He opened Bolan's door for him. "Afternoon, Belasko!"

"Good afternoon, Corporal."

Samuel's grin widened. "Your girlfriend has been asking about you."

Bolan rolled his eyes. He wasn't going to explain for the hundredth time that Cecilia Perez wasn't his girlfriend. "Is the station chief here?"

"Yes, sir. He's waiting for you on the second floor. I'll escort you."

The two men entered the embassy. Corporal Samuels led him upstairs, into a small study. A short stout man with black hair and black eyes stood and held out his hand. "Hello, my name is Ortega. I'm sorry we didn't get a chance to meet before, but this crisis is keeping us very busy." He smiled affably. "I guess I should call you Belasko."

Bolan shook Ortega's hand. "That'll do."

"Well, it looks like we have a war on our hands."

Bolan nodded. "How are the diplomats doing?"

"Pretty damn poorly, but you can't blame them. There really isn't anything for them to do. England has a task force heading toward the Falklands. They say they'll engage any Argentine surface vessel or submarine they encounter. They intend to land on the Falklands, and they'll engage any foreign soldiers they find there. There's been some talk of trying to airlift some United Nations peacekeeping troops onto the Islands, but no one is volunteering."

"What's the Argentine military doing?"

Ortega looked grim. "They're trying to keep it hushed up, but their own task force will sail tomorrow. They're sending every surface combatant they have and every tub that's seaworthy is being crammed with men and materials. They plan to take the Falklands again and this time they intend to hold it. Barring some kind of disaster, they should get there well ahead of the British. The United Kingdom has a reinforced infantry battalion stationed on the islands already. The Argentines are loading a lot of artillery and armored vehicles, and with all of the commercial ships they are impressing as troop carriers, they'll be hitting the Islands in division strength. They should overwhelm the British garrison in time to fortify their position and meet the British fleet, but it's still going to be a hell of a fight."

Bolan looked at the world map on the wall. Red pushpins marked the advance of the British naval task force as it sailed south toward the Falkland Islands. Blue pushpins were clustered around Puerto Bel Grano on the Argentine coast. Tomorrow those pushpins would be moving east.

Station Chief Ortega suddenly dropped his grim demeanor and smiled. "Your girlfriend is asking about you."

Bolan let out a heavy sigh. "Well, maybe I should go see her."

Ortega grinned. "You have about an hour before I get my call from the Pentagon, and then I'll tell you anything new that comes up. Why don't you go say hi to her? She's been cooped up here for days and no one's really been able to pay that much attention to her, except the Marines, and all she does is ask them about you. She said she got her mother sent off to Patagonia, so she's pretty much been incommunicado with any of her friends or family. She's been getting a little frantic."

Bolan rose. He didn't intend to leave the embassy until nightfall, and that was six hours away. There were worse things to do with a spare hour than console a beautiful woman. "Where is she?"

"We gave her a room of her own. I'll show you."

Ortega led Bolan down the hallway past several doors. He stopped and knocked at one. Perez's voice came back. "Yes, what is it?"

"I have someone here who wants to see you."

"Who?"

"Who do you think?"

Feet pounded on the floor and the door flung open. Perez looked utterly ravishing. She flung herself into Bolan's arms and immediately burst into tears. "I thought you were dead!"

Ortega raised his eyebrows at Bolan. "I'll let you two have some privacy. I'll be in the study if you need me for anything."

Perez stepped back and blushed. "I have embarrassed you."

Bolan smiled. "No, not at all. How have you been holding up?"

Her shoulders rose and fell. "It's lonely. I miss my friends. I'm worried about my mother."

"Where did you send her?"

"Patagonia. It's where she grew up. She has old friends near the coast. One would have to be at least sixty years old to know about them. It was the safest place I could think of."

"It sounds like you took very good care of her."

"Thank you." Her eyes shot back to the open door of her room. "Would you like to come in?" She suddenly blushed again, and it did marvelous things to her olive complexion. "I mean, for a minute or two, just so we can talk or something. I just feel all alone. I know I'm safe here, but it's still frightening, if you know what I mean."

Bolan knew all too well what it was like to be alone and surrounded by unseen enemies. "I understand completely."

Perez smiled shyly and led Bolan into her room. It was small, with a single bed along one wall and a desk with a computer on it. Every inch of table space not taken up by the computer was usurped by cosmetics. Rows of hairspray, skin moisturizers and makeup stood ranked from shortest to tallest. Bolan thought she would be stunning without makeup.

Perez smiled demurely. "Would you like something to drink?"

"Sure, what have you got?"

"I have beer." She smiled. "I asked for beer and none of the staff seemed able to help me. Then I asked one of the Marines." She opened the little refrigerator in the corner. Jumbo-sized bottles of Quilmes jammed every cubic inch of space. There had to be two full cases worth.

Bolan smiled. When a beautiful woman told a United States Marine she needed beer, she was going to get beer. "I'll split one with you."

"Fine."

Perez pulled one of the big brown bottles from the fridge

and took a magnetic bottle opener from the door. "What shall we drink to?"

Bolan took the glass of beer. "Peace on earth, and goodwill toward man."

Perez's face grew solemn. Her country was on the brink of war. She raised her glass. "Peace on earth, and goodwill toward man."

The soldier raised his glass. His hand stopped as his lips touched the foam. His instincts kicked into action.

Perez's nose wrinkled fetchingly. "Is something wrong?"

Bolan's eyes darted to the table behind her. Her rows of cosmetics sat in their lines. A jar of moisturizing cream was open with its coral-colored top next to it. Bolan's eyes widened as he rose from the bed.

Perez flung her glass at his eyes.

The Executioner brought up his hand and the beer glass shattered against his knuckles. Beer splattered his hair and brow but his eyes remained clear. Perez leaped back and moved to the computer table. She picked up a hairbrush, bit into the bristles with her teeth and yanked the handle with her hand. A five-inch stiletto of blue steel gleamed dully as it shot toward Bolan's throat.

The soldier brought up his bloodied left hand to chop at her wrist. Perez's knife hand writhed like a snake and switched from a stab to a slash in midstrike. The cold burn of steel sank through Bolan's forearm. The Executioner accepted the damage. His right hand whipped in an arc and chopped into the woman's inner elbow like an ax.

The knife flew out of her hand as her arm spasmed. Bolan lurched backward. The average human would have sunk to their knees clutching their paralyzed arm from the hand strike. Perez's foot rose without hesitation. Bolan rolled back with the blow as her heel clipped his chin. The blow was heavy but he managed to avoid most of its force, yet it gave Perez a split second to work with. She didn't lunge. She jumped backward and scooped again at the cosmetics on the computer table. Her right arm hung useless at her side but her left grabbed the can of hairspray. She slapped the can against her thigh and smashed off the aerosol can's cap.

Her left hand shot forward and depressed the spray nozzle. Bolan yanked his head out of the way as the can hissed at him.

No perfume or mist of hairspray projected from the aerosol propellant. There was no scent at all. Air rippled where his head had just been as something invisible sprayed forth.

Bolan continued his lunge past Perez and rolled on his shoulder across the floor. He rolled to one knee and tore the 9 mm Beretta 93-R out of its holster.

Perez hadn't followed Bolan for a second attempt. She lunged through the doorway and slammed the door shut behind her. Bolan rose. There was a shout of consternation in the hall outside and the thud of a body falling. Bolan yanked open the door with a bloody hand and came into the hall leading with his machine pistol. CIA Station Chief Ortega lay on the carpet in the middle of the hallway. His brown face was white as a sheet and his lips had turned purple. Bolan's nostrils flared. There had been no smell from the spray when she had shot it at his face, but there was an ugly odor in the hallway that Bolan knew from long experience. It was the smell of bitter almonds—cyanide gas.

People had begun screaming.

Bolan ran down the hall and leaped down the stairs five at a time. He hit the landing where a group of embassy workers were gathered around one of their colleagues, who lay on the floor in the same state as Ortega. Several people saw the gun in the soldier's hand and the screaming began afresh. Bolan plunged past them toward the front door. He ran down the stairs to the driveway. Two Marine Corps Embassy Guards lay on the ground. One was pale and motionless and the second one's death convulsions were just beginning to quiet.

Corporal Samuels sat on the driveway. Blood poured down his face from his split left eyebrow. He looked stunned, but other than that he looked very much alive.

The embassy's automatic gates were closing. Bolan caught a glimpse of Perez. Brakes screamed and cars fishtailed as she ran through traffic. Bolan's run changed to a leap as the wrought iron gate slammed shut before him. He put a foot on one of the crossbars and grabbed a top spike of the gate with his free hand. Bolan vaulted over the top of the gate and landed on the pavement beyond with bone-jarring force. He rose and swept the street.

Perez was gone. It was lunch hour and the sidewalks were crowded. Pedestrians on both sides of the street stared at the bloodied man with the gun in his hand. No one was looking backward to where the woman had run. He had everyone's full attention. Bolan turned back to the gate. "Corporal, let me in."

Samuels rose unsteadily and triggered the gate. Bolan pulled out his handkerchief and handed it to the big Marine. "Are you all right?"

Samuels pressed the handkerchief to his brow. He was still shaky on his feet. He suddenly snapped to attention. "Damn it! Preston! McManus!"

He whirled to look at his men.

Bolan shook his head. "They're dead. She used cyanide. They died in seconds."

Samuels gaped. "She had a can. She sprayed them both in the face and they went down. She tried to spray me but nothing came out. I went for my gun and—"

Bolan could guess what happened. "And she nearly took your head off."

"Damn right." Samuels shook his head again to clear it. "I'm a brown belt and I've never seen anyone kick like that. Hell, I never even saw it coming."

Bolan saw the can of hairspray where it had rolled against the tire of an embassy car. "Corporal?"

Samuels looked around dazedly. "Yeah? I mean, yes sir?"

"We've got two down out here and two more inside. The station chief is one of them. Police the area. Get some men and bag the bodies. Then find a field agent if there are any on the premises and have him go over every square inch of the room Perez was in. Be careful of her cosmetics. She seems to have had a number of poisons in her possession."

Samuels eyes cleared. "Yes, sir. I'm on it."

Bolan stared out at the street. The woman had carried at least two different forms of poison concealed in her belongings. She was adept at knife fighting. She was obviously a trained assassin. By the way she had clocked Samuels she was also obviously a martial artist. Bolan grimaced and rubbed his chin.

He thought he had a good idea just what that martial art might be.

18

Barbara Price sounded very unhappy over the secure phone. "The President isn't happy, Striker. He gave implicit instructions that no CIA assets were to be used, other than in an advisory and tactical information resource role."

"He didn't go active. He was walking down the hall of the American Embassy when he took a faceful of cyanide."

"I know that," the Farm's mission controller replied. "Hal knows that. The President knows that, too."

"But the CIA station chief in Argentina is dead, along with an embassy intern and two United States Marines." Bolan's eyes rested on the wall, but his gaze looked far into the distance. He didn't like what he saw. "I'm the one that brought the woman there. I take full responsibility. Does the President want me to withdraw from this operation?"

"No, it's just…"

Bolan sighed heavily. "It's just that four good men are dead, and nothing is going to bring them back."

"You're not going to be recalled, Mack, but I don't know how much more support you're going to get on this one. The director of the CIA wants to know what's going on down there and why his station chief is dead. There's pressure to call the whole thing off."

"And just let the war happen?"

"That's what Hal said. That's why you're not on a plane."

Bolan looked down. The doctor had put seven stitches in his forearm. "Did you get a description of the woman?"

"We did. We know that her name isn't Cecilia Perez. Her paperwork was impressive, and we were hampered by the fact that Akira had to break into the Argentine police computers, but they have no record of such a woman. Either as a criminal or a civilian. She's an undercover agent of some kind."

Bolan thought about the way she had fought. He hadn't seen it, but he thought about how she had kicked a six-foot-six Marine in the jaw and almost knocked him unconscious. That required a good deal of flexibility, power and elevation. He thought about the musical intruments he had seen in Nico Souza's house and the machetes on the walls. "She won't be in any files in Argentina, but we might have more luck trying Brazil."

"What makes you say that?"

"The way she fought. I think she was trained in *capoeira*."

"What?"

"It's a Brazilian martial art. Very acrobatic. The same stuff that Souza practices. The woman took off a United States Marine's head with her foot. She came real close to taking off mine as well."

"Okay, but that's not a lot to go on."

"Try looking in the region of Bahia. The Bear told me that's the real hotbed of the art. He told me it used to have a reputation as the fighting style of a lot of street gangs."

"Okay, an unidentified woman, black hair, black eyes, olive complexion, trained martial artist, possible origin in Bahia, Brazil."

That sounded thin even to Bolan. "Try to tie in Souza. He has to have some kind of record to be this high up in things."

"Now that's actually helpful. Have you got anything else?"

"She came at me with an aerosol can full of cyanide. She also tried to poison me with something in a drink. We don't have the equipment to analyze it here. I have samples flying to you right now. I'm also sending some to Dr. Lopez." A bell went off in Bolan's head. "Did Bear find out anything about the poison samples we sent him that killed the men from the morgue?"

"I faxed that information to the safehouse an hour ago. Akira should have it now."

"Can you call it up on your computer?"

"Give me a minute." Bolan could hear the tapping of keys across the link. "Yes. Lopez was correct in his assumption. It was a botanical toxin, from a plant. It acts much like a blood agent, if it's introduced into your system through the soft tissues, it goes right into your bloodstream. It would attack your nervous system and kill you almost immediately. If no one knew what it was it would look like a violent seizure. Also, being a botanical poison, it breaks down in the body very quickly. The samples Bear got were pretty degraded, but he worked on them using Lopez's theory as a guide. He's seventy-five percent sure of what he has."

Bolan allowed himself a faint ray of hope. "It's not found in the Amazon rain forest, is it?"

Barbara paused a moment. "No, it's found in Bahia, in the highlands. Some of the practitioners of the West African religions use it in tiny amounts in some of their ceremonies. They also use it occasionally to kill each other."

"What did Bear find out about the Indians in the region?"

"Well, Bahia's not part of the Brazilian rain forest as we think of it. It's on the coast, but it goes pretty deep into the continent, and there are lots of forests and mountains. It was where the Portuguese captured most of the African slaves and set up the major plantations. The majority of the Indians were wiped out or civilized. There are cultural revival movements there, and plenty of the indigenous peoples of the area are in isolated villages, slums or reservations."

"Have Bear and Akira see about breaking into the Brazilian police records. Find out everything you can about Souza, and try to tie the woman to him."

"The CIA branch in Brazil has already been working on Souza. Let me pull up what we have." There was a moment's pause. "We know he has a criminal record, but it has been sealed. It appears that people in the government and the police are protecting him. Supposedly, he's a legitimate businessman these days. He has a multimillion-dollar empire, and it seems he pays his taxes."

"Let me guess. Import-export."

Price laughed. Just about every drug trafficker in the world who had a "legitimate" business as a front had something to do with the import-export trade. It was very convenient for business. "You got it."

"Find out if he has a house or owns land in Bahia. Find out everything you can about his business interests. See if any of them lead to the Bahia highlands."

"I'm on it."

"Have the CIA in São Paulo heard anything from the tracers?"

"Not a thing. Either they've been discovered and destroyed, or they are out of range."

"How much more battery life do they have?"

"They're the best the Pentagon could come up with, but even so they are small, and their batteries are smaller. According to Aaron they've got a day of function left, possibly two if they don't get cold."

"Does the CIA have any assets in Bahia?"

"I just don't know. I doubt it. Why, you think he might be there?"

Bolan looked down at his forearm again. "It's a hunch, slim one, but we have some tenuous leads that point in that direction. At the moment I have nothing else to go on."

"I don't know if I can get any CIA assets authorized to go to Bahia."

"Don't bother. The bad guys have to have people watching the embassy, waiting for me to leave. Rather than playing musical cabs, I think I'll just go straight to the airport. Have a plane ready for me. Then get one ready for the rest of the team. Have them leave the safehouse and take off an hour after I do. Have them bring a pair of receivers and a full warload. I need a safehouse in Bahia, in the capital.''

"That's Salvador. I'll see what I can arrange, but it could take a little time."

Bolan stood. "I need to be airborne in forty-five minutes."

*Buenos Aires, Argentina*

WALDEMAR SALOME looked at the assassin. Her eyes were wild and her chest heaved. Cecilia Perez was clearly enraged.

"I had him! I swear to God. I had him!"

Salome steepled his fingers before him on the desk. "Yes, I'm sure you did. He's proving to be very resourceful."

"What are you going to do about him?"

Salome had spent a great deal of time thinking about that. "At the moment, nothing."

"Nothing!"

"Nothing. The Argentine fleet is about to invade the Falkland Islands. In little more than a week the British task force will be in range to engage it. At that time, I'll sink the majority of the task force. What is left will be crippled, and unable to stand up to the Argentine fleet. The Falkland Islands will become the sovereign soil of Argentina. It will be a tremendous victory. In cowardly and spiteful retaliation, the British will seem to have the Argentine president assassinated. Our friend the general will have the military declare martial law and temporarily take power. There will be purges in the government. Many corrupt politicians will be brought to trial. The general will be hailed as a hero and the savior of the nation. It will be sad when he, too, falls to an assassin's bullet. Then someone with less ambition and more gratitude will take his place. Someone more tractable. Then we'll see what we can do with an entire nation at our disposal."

Perez was implacable. "I want the American dead." She held up her arm. Her fingers and thumb stuck out of a short cast encasing her forearm. "Look at this! The bastard fractured my ulna. It will be months before I can use my arm properly."

Salome sympathized, but there was little that could be done about it at the moment short of having every shooter they could find in Buenos Aires assault the United States Embassy. "Trying to kill him now would be a terrible risk. We must wait until he exposes himself, and even then, I fear if he does it would be an attempt to draw us out into a trap. Forget the American, for the moment. Without Nico he has run out of leads. There's nothing he can do except watch the war on CNN. We'll simply let him fail in his mission and watch us succeed. That will be a terrible punishment for a man like him. Later, if we can find out where he's operating from or who he is and who he works for, we'll kill him, his family, his friends and anyone else connected to him."

"I don't like it. I don't like him. He's a danger to us as long as he draws breath. We must kill him immediately. Drive a truck bomb into the American Embassy if we must, but kill him."

Salome's voice grew firm. "Now is not the time for rash action. We need time to let the plan unfold."

"You're right. You're always right," she answered, but her voice told him she didn't believe it.

"You killed the CIA station chief?"

"I sprayed cyanide up his nose. Where is the subtlety in that?"

Salome suppressed a frown. It bothered him that she was insane. He sought something to placate her. "When it is time, you may kill the general."

The woman snorted derisively. "He's a pig."

"You don't want to kill the general?"

"I want to kill him very much. I'll enjoy it, like I enjoyed killing the British and Argentine ambassadors. I like killing everyone you ask me to. You know that, Waldemar. It's just that the idea of killing the American holds a special place in my heart."

"I understand."

"You're the only person who ever has." Her mind suddenly switched gears. "How's Nico?"

"He's here. It was too hot in São Paulo. I thought it safest to have him brought to me." Salome smiled. "He wants to see you."

Perez's face was unreadable. "Do you want me to see him?"

"Don't you want to?"

"No, I mean, do you want me to kill him?"

Salome blinked.

Perez looked at him in mild exasperation. "The American found him, got to him, escaped his trap and left him for dead. Nico has been compromised. Do you want me to kill him?"

Salome stared at her for several long moments. She stared back impassively and waited for his answer. A slow smile spread across his face. It was moments like this that made him realize, more than anything else, that he trusted her more than any person on earth. She had only one loyalty, and that was to him.

"No, do not kill Nico." Salome turned to stare at the map on the wall. "Not yet."

**19**

*Salvador, Brazil*

The late afternoon breeze brought in tiny whitecaps with the surf and stirred the palm trees. The sand was soft, and the sky and the sea were so blue it nearly hurt the eyes. Bahia was beautiful. Bolan sat at an outside table and drank Xingu black beer. It was darker than any English stout he had encountered, but it was nowhere near as thick or bitter. Schwarz, Grimaldi, McCarter and Encizo walked up to the table. The mood of the men was dark.

Encizo looked at Bolan's arm. "Looks like she got a piece of you."

The soldier nodded. "She got a big piece of the embassy."

"We heard." McCarter looked at Bolan and frankly stated, "They got to Tito."

Bolan met his gaze. "Dr. Lopez?"

"Yeah. He went back to police headquarters. He wanted to ask some of his colleagues among the inspectors if they had any knowledge of Souza's activities in Brazil."

"How?"

"They got him in his office. It looks like someone put something in his coffee. Two other inspectors were killed in the same fashion. We're not sure if they were killed because they knew something or they drank out of the same urn as Tito."

Bolan stared out at the surf. "You have the receiver?"

Gadgets Schwarz held up a small aluminum suitcase. "Right here."

The soldier eyed his friend. "How's your head?"

"It aches."

"Let's see what we have."

Schwarz put the case down on the table and flipped it open. The receiver was really little more than a sophisticated radio with a very powerful antenna. The electronics ace pulled up the antenna loop and began flipping a knob. He stopped almost immediately.

"You have something?"

Schwarz grinned. "I've got the transmitter we put in the phone." He flipped his dial slightly to switch frequencies. "I have the transmitter we put in Souza's wallet as well." His grin turned feral as he looked at his display. "They're on the same line. I've got a bearing of due north. Signal strength indicates the transmitters are approximately three miles away."

Bolan looked north up the white sand of the Bahia coastline. "A beach house."

"Probably, but we'll need a second bearing to triangulate."

"You have a second receiver."

"It's with the weapons."

"Good, take McCarter and head about two miles west into town and start heading north. Jack, Rafe and I are going to take a little drive up the coastal road. If Souza is hiding out, I suspect it will be in a house not traceable to him. We leave in half an hour."

Bolan rose and took his suitcase with the satellite link. He went down to a cabana and pulled the striped awning closed. Babara Price answered his call immediately.

"I have some information for you."

"Shoot."

"In Souza's youth he was part of a street gang in Salvador called the Torroros. They studied *capoeira*, and they fought the other neighborhood gangs. He was one of the leaders and was arrested for numerous assaults and petty crimes. He was supposedly involved in some killings. He rose above gang-level of crime and began to run guns into the Brazilian interior. He had a partner, a Waldemar Salome. Salome had a younger sister, Cecilia. She was arrested for murder in Bahia but released after the witnesses disappeared. Her description matches the woman in Buenos Aires.''

Bolan thought about that. ''What happened to her brother?''

''According to Brazilian police records, he's dead. He was involved in a gun battle with police boats on the Sobradinho.''

''Let me guess, his body was never recovered.''

''That's right. Soon after, the police in Bahia stopped going after Souza. He supposedly went legit. Like I told you before, most of the files on him are sealed.''

''People have been paid. He's being protected. Souza's business was the front while Salome continued the illegal side of it. Being dead made him hard to investigate and hard to arrest. Everyone we've come across up until now has been a cutout or an intermediary. If Souza and Salome were into gunrunning, they have probably been trading Russian black-market weapons. Somehow they lucked into or came into contact with someone who had access to the antishipping prototypes. Drug money paid for the experimental hardware they've been using.''

Price was quiet for a moment. ''You're thinking that a pair of street thugs from the poorest slum in Brazil have risen to starting international wars and toppling foreign governments?''

Bolan smiled grimly. ''Initially, it's a bit of a leap, but street thugs are hungry, and trained martial artists are men and women of great willpower and determination. Every step of the way they have seized opportunities, had other people do their fighting for them, and when the situation called for it, they struck with utter ruthlessness. We're dealing with criminal brilliance. Playing one gang against another, paying off police and petty officials were all things they learned in the streets. They've simply taken those lessons and elevated them to the international level. We're dealing with people who started with nothing and are taking a brilliant stab at ending up owning a nation."

"How do you want to play it?"

"I'm going to take down Souza, right now. He'll lead me to Salome."

"Hal can get you some backup."

"There's no time. Gadgets says the batteries in the tracers could go at any time. We won't get another shot at this. I'm going to triangulate on Souza and go through his front door in twenty minutes."

THE EXECUTIONER sat on his heels in the sand and examined the house. It was on an isolated strip of beach. It was a long and low affair of white walls and Spanish tiles. The whitewashed wall was low enough to vault, and the approach from the sea was open. The beach was a sharp crescent forming a tiny bay. A wooden dock marched into the ocean on wooden pilings, and a decent-sized yacht that was too big for the little wooden pier was moored fifty yards from shore in the still, blue water. Palm trees grew thick and lush and leaned out over the sand. Deeper in the palms a landing pad for helicopters had been cleared and the ground had been tamped down. The pad was empty now and completely concealed from both the beach road and the ocean. The house and the landscape around it were stunningly beautiful. Bolan spoke into his mike. "Is everyone in position?"

McCarter's voice came back. "Roger that. We're in position."

"Let's do it." Bolan rose off his heels and flicked the

safety off his 9 mm Colt submachine gun and flipped up the ladder sight of the grenade launcher. He pulled his gas mask down over his face and squeezed the M-203's trigger.

The butt of the submachine gun recoiled into Bolan's shoulder as the 40 mm tear gas grenade arced out of the launcher's muzzle and looped into a window of the house, shattering its glass. Bolan racked the breech as he heard the weapons of Schwarz, Encizo, and McCarter go off. He loaded another gas grenade and fired into a window that faced the sea.

A man in a white suit burst onto the back porch through the thickening cloud of gas. He brandished a heavy FN NATO assault rifle in his hands. Bolan raised his own weapon and sent a 3-round burst into the man's chest. The man staggered and turned to search the beach with streaming eyes. His skin was dark bronze and his face had the eyes and hooked nose of a native Indian. He raised his heavy rifle without hesitation and fired a burst at Bolan.

The sonic cracks of the rifle's bullets whipped the air and the bullets themselves tore past through the palms. The Executioner put another burst into the man and the gunner again returned fire. Bullets scudded into the sand at Bolan's feet. Only the hardman's tearing eyes kept him from hitting his target. Bolan raised his aim. The man was either on drugs or wearing body armor beneath his white suit. Either way, body shots from the Colt's subsonic 9 mm hollowpoints weren't stopping him. There was no guarantee Bolan's own armor would stop the bullets of the rifle he faced. The gunner's rifle snarled at him again. Bolan took an extra split second to aim, then squeezed his trigger. The man's head snapped back on his shoulders and he fell to the porch where the spreading gas obscured him.

Bolan loaded a frag into the breech of his grenade launcher.

Another man in a white suit leaped onto the porch. His weapon swept the beach on full auto but his long burst was high and wide of the mark. The gas filling the porch and spilling out of the house was too thick for a decent head shot, and Bolan couldn't stand and exchange fire with the heavy rifle. He fired his grenade launcher and threw himself to the sand.

The grenade detonated on the porch. Yellow fire flashed in the gray smoke of the tear gas and the rifleman twisted and fell.

Bolan loaded another tear gas grenade as he rose and fired it into the house. He slid another frag into the smoking breech and slung the Colt carbine. He drew his Desert Eagle semi-automatic pistol. Whoever the riflemen in the white suits were, they were hard-chargers and they were armored. At house-clearing distances, the .44 Magnum's steel-jacketed armor-piercing solids would even the odds.

Bolan moved to the porch and tried to scan through the choking gas that poured out of the house. The darkened interior was lit by orange flashes and the house reverberated with automatic rifle fire.

"Rafe, what have you got?"

"Heavy resistance! Jack and I have set a charge! We're making our own door!"

Bolan crouched. A second later the whole house shook as Encizo made his own entry through one of the clay-brick exterior walls. Bolan moved across the porch and entered through the choking clouds of gas. Another gunner staggered into view. Within the confines of the house the concentration of gas was close to asphyxiating. He emptied his rifle in the vague direction of the porch. The Desert Eagle rolled twice in Bolan's hands and hammered the man down.

"McCarter! What have you got!"

"We're in the foyer! Four hostiles down! No sign of Souza or Perez!"

Bolan moved through the room and down the hall the gunman had come from. There was a closed door and Bolan fired a shot into it and rolled aside. Answering fire tore through the door and ripped into the wall of the hallway.

Bolan holstered the hand cannon and whipped his carbine back around on its sling. He stepped past the door and fired. The frag punched through the thin interior door and detonated. The door rattled on its hinges as steel fragments struck it like hail. The Executioner stepped back in front of the door and put his boot to it. The door flung open on its hinges. Two of the hardmen lay on the ground. Bolan looked at the face of the third man. His head was already heavily bandaged. Blood from new head wounds stained the carpet where he lay.

"This is Striker! Souza is down! Repeat, Souza is down!"

Schwarz's voice came back. "Roger that, we are—" He made a grunt over the radio and his voice went dead.

"Gadgets!"

The Executioner moved down the hall. It opened into another gas-filled room. Beyond it lay another door with light streaming in through small windows. Bolan burst through it. The architecture of the house was colonial Portuguese and it had the traditional interior courtyard. There was a small fountain and a table with graceful wrought iron chairs. Gadgets Schwarz lay facedown on the tiles. Cecilia Perez stood over him and was struggling to pull his carbine from where it was slung across his body.

She looked up as Bolan strode forward.

Her dark eyes were bloodshot from the gas and insane with hate. She dropped the carbine and leaped over Schwarz's body. She came forward weaving from side to side in the lethal pattern of her art.

A part of Bolan burned to gun her down. She had ruthlessly murdered good men. But Nico Souza lay dead and she was the only link Bolan had to her brother. He needed her alive.

Her hands came up as she closed. Bolan dropped the Colt on its sling. He couldn't afford to exchange punches and kicks with her. To do so would be lethally foolish even under the best conditions, but he wasn't going to play by her rules.

The soldier stepped in and seized one of the wrought iron chairs as he passed it. The stitches in his arm pulled and tore with the strain. Perez skidded to a halt and her eyes flared as Bolan whipped the iron chair up over his head. The woman twisted and tried to dodge. A kick or a punch she could easily have slipped with the grace of an acrobat, but the chair was too big and she had charged too close too fast. Bolan brought the wrought iron chair down.

Perez was swatted to the tiles with bone-breaking force.

"Rafe! What's the situation?"

"No hostiles active. We're continuing to sweep the house."

"I have the woman. Gadgets is down. We extract now. Rafe, get to the yacht and get her started. Jack, give me a hand. McCarter! Take position on the back porch and cover us."

A moment later Grimaldi burst onto the patio. He knelt beside Schwarz and peered into his eyes through his gas mask, then he quickly checked him for bullet holes. He looked up. "He doesn't seem to be wounded. He's breathing but unconscious, I'd say your girlfriend clocked him."

"Get him up, let's get out of here."

Perez moaned as Bolan pulled her up and heaved her over his shoulder. Grimaldi staggered under Schwarz's weight and Bolan gave the pilot his free shoulder to help with Gadgets. The two of them staggered out of the house under the weight of the bodies.

McCarter waited by the porch with his weapon leveled. Bolan glanced past him. Encizo was already swimming to the yacht. He had left the motorboat for transporting Schwarz and the woman. They retreated as a unit down to the dock. No more riflemen poured out of the house, only the gray-white smoke of tear gas.

They loaded Schwarz and the woman into the motorboat. Encizo had brought the communication gear with him and left it in the boat. The motor turned over and they tooled out to the yacht. The engines smoked to life with a roar and Bolan, McCarter and Grimaldi manhandled the bodies on board. They took them inside the cabin as McCarter hauled in the anchor.

Bolan pulled off Schwarz's mask and peered into his eyes. The electronics ace coughed and his eyes rolled. "What happened?"

"Where are you?"

Schwarz focused on Bolan fuzzily. "What?"

"Who am I?"

"Who are you?"

Bolan and Grimaldi exchanged frowns. If Schwarz hadn't had a concussion before, he very likely had one now. Bolan looked at Perez where she lay at Grimaldi's knees. She moaned as the pilot ran a thumb over her skull. "How is she?"

Grimaldi shrugged. "She's got a big ol' lump on the side of her head, and you broke her collarbone. Nothing fatal."

The engines surged as Encizo pulled the yacht out of the little bay. He yelled back from the bridge. "Where do you want me to take this tub?"

Bolan gave that some thought. Souza's neighbors would have heard the noise. The police would already be on the way. It was anybody's guess whether they would know if the yacht was supposed to be missing or not. Buenos Aires was a long boat ride away, and the Brazilian coast guard might well be on the lookout for them. No port along the coast would be safe.

"Take us straight out to sea. We'll get on the horn. With the crisis in the South Atlantic we have to have some submarines lurking about. We'll see about setting up a rendezvous and scuttling the yacht."

"You've got it. Heading out due east."

Grimaldi pondered. "Well, we have at least a day or two on this boat, probably three or four, then."

Bolan frowned. The pilot was right, and with the British task force steaming in, it was three or four days they couldn't afford if they were to have any chance at all of stopping the war.

"We have the satellite link. We have Cecilia. I think we should have a talk with Kurtzman." He looked at the female assassin without emotion. "Then maybe we should give her brother a call."

Grimaldi finished patting her down for weapons. His face split into a grin as he pulled an envelope out of her pocket.

"What is it?"

Grimaldi pulled open the envelope and his grin turned triumphant. "Airline tickets."

## 20

*South Atlantic Ocean*

Mack Bolan sat in the secure communications room of the
United States 688-class nuclear attack submarine *Corpus
Christi*. It was running at antennae depth and her communications suite was one of the most sophisticated at sea. The
link with Stony Man Farm was crystal clear.

Aaron Kurtzman sounded happy. "I've had a thought."

"Oh?"

"Well, I've been thinking about the parameters you gave
me. The weapon we hypothesized had to be able to reach out
and hit the *Capitan Prat* in Drake Passage, the *Manchester,
Boxer* and *Battle-axe* off the Falklands, and it had to be able
to hit *Aspero* and *Hercules* in Puerto Bel Grano in
Argentina."

"Yeah, I admit it was an ugly set of parameters."

"They were. Too ugly for any conventional weapon system. So I had to start thinking unconventionally. I looked at
the photos and I listened to radio communication tapes of
*Battle-axe* before she went down. It all came down to a question of verticality."

"You're saying they were all hit topside."

"From an almost ninety-degree angle. Both *Aspero* and
*Hercules* were blown open like exploded beer cans. Something punched through their top decks and shattered them
from the inside. That got me thinking. Then I listened to the

tapes of *Battle-axe*'s last moments. *Manchester* and *Boxer* went down almost before they knew what hit them. Even with two ships burning, *Battle-axe* could barely pick up what was coming at her before it was too late. She tried to use both infrared and radar-guided missiles. Both failed to target. She tried to use her guns at the last second but she couldn't get enough elevation.

"It's brilliant, really. Most naval radars sweep up and out in great arcs in all directions, but directly above the radar there is a cone where no radar waves are transmitted. It's like being in the eye of the radar's hurricane or a blind spot. Naval radars can detect planes or missiles high up in the atmosphere, that's why most antiship weapons are cruise missiles that skim low over the water to try to get in under the enemy radar. They only pop up at the last second to attack. The weapon we're looking at is coming in straight down."

Bolan frowned. "Okay, I'll buy that, but it still doesn't explain how it gets above its target. It can't fly low and suddenly pop up to a vertical altitude without being detected. That I don't buy, and we've already ruled out stolen B-2 stealth bombers dropping bombs."

Kurtzman's excitement grew. "Now, thinking B-2 stealth bombers is wrong, but you're getting warmer."

The soldier's frown deepened. "Bear, even if they have some kind of seagoing SCUD missile system, it has to fire from somewhere and have an arc of trajectory. Even if no one detected it when it was launching, modern radar would still see it coming in long before it got vertical above its target."

"Striker, you're almost there. You're red hot."

Bolan spoke half in jest. "What you're talking about is an intercontinental ballistic missile?"

"Bingo!"

Bolan stared at the speaker system. "An ICBM?"

"Think about it, everything you've said is right. The

launch of even something like a SCUD would be detected, and its flight would be seen by radar before it could go vertical. A cruise missile flying low still has to pop up to attack. But an ICBM, Striker, that allows you to attack from a launch site a thousand miles from your target, two thousand miles, hell, six thousand miles or more depending on the make and model. Your launch site is so far from your target that no one on the planet knows you've launched anything, least of all the helpless souls you're firing upon." Kurtzman paused to take an excited breath. "And here's the real kicker. Your target's warning radar doesn't see the weapon come in until it's too late, because the weapon is literally coming down on them. Straight down out of space."

It was a startling thought. "All right, but then how does it evade targeting radars, and why doesn't infrared pick up the signature of its rocket engine as it comes in?"

"Well the radar is easy, the weapon carries its own onboard electronic warfare suite. It jams its target's radar when it goes into attack mode."

"So why doesn't its engines give off heat signatures?"

Kurtzman sounded positively smug. "It doesn't have any engines."

"I thought we were talking about an intercontinental ballistic missile, Bear. They have great big engines."

"Ah, yes, they certainly do. But you're talking about the booster, I'm talking about the payload."

"You're saying the missile section falls away."

"Of course. Think about it. We're talking about going up into space and then coming back down. When the payload reenters the atmosphere, it could be doing up to Mach 20. It doesn't need any more speed. It's got all the speed it could ever need. As a matter of fact, it needs to slow down. When the weapon hits the upper atmosphere at double-digit Mach numbers, it sets off huge shock waves. The air around it gets sucked into the shock wave and superheated into electrified plasma. The weapon's own targeting radar can't see through the heat and electricity generated by the shock waves, so it has to slow down or go in blind. Also, the weapon has to maneuver to hit its target. To do that, it needs stub wings or fins. At those speeds, wings would rip off. I'm betting the weapon has some forward firing rockets it uses to slow itself to more manageable speeds, say around Mach 6 or so. Then the rockets fall away, its wings slide out of the fuselage, and boom, you have it. A glider, coming in ballistically at Mach 6, without rockets or ramjets for infrared sensors to detect, and the heat from reentry would be cooling down by the millisecond. Its own onboard electronic warfare system jams the early warning radar and radar guidance of the defensive missile systems. It's also coming in nearly vertical, so radar doesn't detect it until it's too late, anyway. The weapon doesn't have to be that big, either. Since there are no rocket engines or jets, you have a lot more room for guidance, countermeasures and payload. Coming in vertically, you hit a ship where it's thinnest. Most of a ship's armor is on its sides and keel. Coming in straight down, you rip through the top decks and plunge amidships. You gut the vessel from inside and break her spine.''

''Sounds a little expensive.''

''Not as expensive as you might think. All the technology is available. Intercontinental ballistic rocket boosters are expensive, but, let's say you're using an older model that's going to be scrapped as obsolete. You get double duty out of the booster, first for nuclear weapon delivery, and then when you develop more accurate missiles for your nukes, you put the antiship warheads on the old ones, which only have to get the weapons boosted into the general target area. There they detach and find the target themselves. It's actually a fine bit of recycling.''

Bolan had to admit he was impressed. He had given Kurtzman what seemed to be an impossible set of weapon parameters, and he had found a simple solution. "All right, you have me so far, but where are they launching from? You still have to hit the Falkland Islands, Puerto Bel Grano, Argentina and a ship in Drake Passage in the Antarctic Circle. The only way I see it is with a nuclear ballistic submarine, and how did our friends get hold of one of those?"

"Well, now, that was my first conclusion as well, but like you said, how do they get hold of a nuclear ballistic submarine? The only people who sell that kind of equipment or give it to their allies are the Russians, and if they had given away one of their submarines or had it stolen, our intelligence would have heard about it. Plus, even if you buy one, you still need an experienced crew to operate the submarine and manage the missiles. I don't buy that coming together either. That means the weapons system has to be land-based."

Bolan shook his head. "That leaves Argentina. There is an international crisis going on. England's array of surveillance satellites is small, but it's high quality. You know that they'll have at least one or more observation platforms eyeing Argentina all the time. It's highly likely they would detect a missile launch, and we're looking at multiple launches at different times. Plus, we'd be talking about people using ballistic missiles in Argentina against Argentines. An intercontinental ballistic missile launch isn't exactly the easiest thing to hide."

"You're right on both counts, but I've been examining the ranges involved. You could do it and avoid all of the problems you just mentioned, if you launched from Antarctica."

Bolan sat straighter in his chair. "You're right."

"Thank you."

"No, it makes sense. When we captured Cecilia Perez, she had plane tickets to Ushuaia. It's the southernmost city in Argentina. It's the southernmost city in the world before Antarctica."

"How is she? I hear she's a handful."

"She gave Gadgets a concussion. We had her handcuffed

and she had a broken collarbone, and even then when the sailors tried to get her on board the submarine she headbutted one of them and broke his jaw and put her boots into another and shoved him into the drink. The ship's medic set her collarbone and she's cooling her heels in the brig." Bolan switched the subject. "So why hasn't a satellite seen ballistic missile launches in Antarctica?"

Kurtzman sounded vaguely appalled. "For one thing, it's physically impossible to position a satellite permanently over the North or South Poles. Satellites move in orbit around the earth. You can set one to orbit at the same rate as the planet's rotation so it seems to stand still over an area, but that has to be above the equator so it can move with its target. We're talking about Antarctica, which is directly over the axis of the planet. A satellite just can't hover over it. It has to orbit somewhere."

"Oh."

"For that matter, I can't think of any government that routinely has satellites that are dedicated to viewing the South Pole on flyby. There's just nothing there to see but ice. Whoever our friends are, they most likely have a listing of which satellites, if any, do pass over the South Pole so they can time their launches so they won't be seen."

Kurtzman seemed to have an answer for everything, Bolan thought. "So where do they get the boosters and these weapons?"

"That's a touchier subject. The Russians are desperate for hard currency, and they're willing to sell their most advanced weapon systems with little thought of who they're selling them to. However, they're leery about selling nuclear weapons. They're afraid that if they do the entire world will start trade embargoes. No one wants to see Russia's nuclear arsenal sold to the highest bidder and going into the hands of tyrants like Saddam Hussein. However, if someone just wanted to buy obsolete booster systems without buying the nuclear warheads, certain unscrupulous generals in the former Soviet Union might just sell them for hard cash and then declare them destroyed during a round of nuclear disarmament.''

Bolan could see that happening all too easily. "So where do they get the weapon system? Who built it?''

"Well, the United States certainly could have done it. Japan has the technology. So does France, but I think it comes down to the Russians again. You have to remember how things were at the height of the cold war under the Reagan presidency. Our Navy was much more capable than theirs. We were the only Navy in the world that was still fielding battleships. The Russians had nothing that could match them. We also had fifteen of the biggest aircraft carriers the world had ever seen, all of which carried supersonic fighter jets. The best the Russians had were a few half cruiser-half helicopter carrier ships that had some subsonic jump jets. Our fleets were also purposefully built for extended fighting. They had high endurance and were expected to stay at sea for protracted periods of time.

"The Russian naval philosophy was entirely different. They couldn't afford to build battleships or build a true carrier fleet, so they built swarms of heavy cruisers with massive missile armaments. They sacrificed fuel stores, living quarters and every other conceivable amenity to stud their ships with heavy missiles. If it came to a war with the United States, they intended to try to cripple our fleet and bring down our biggest ships with one or two massive salvos of long-range missiles while they kept their own ships out of range of our weapons. Their whole naval strategy depended on wiping us out with one big punch. Given that parameter, if they backed that shipborne missile launch with a barrage of antiship weapons coming down vertically from space at the same time, they would stand a very good chance of succeeding.''

"All right, then how come our intelligence never heard about the plan?"

"That's a good question. I'm betting the Russians never fielded the weapon. We're finding out that the Russians were working on all sorts of weird and wonderful weapons systems right before the Soviet Union fell apart. With the state of their economy since then they've had to massively downsize their armed forces and they've had to scrap many weapons-procurement plans. They've given up on the two big carriers they were trying to build, and their army couldn't afford to bring out the planned successor to the T-80 tank. I'm willing to bet most of their experimental stuff got scrapped."

"So, we're looking at someone with a few million to burn who got hold of a batch of working Russian prototypes, which were lying around in storage."

"That's my best guess. You were the one who postulated that someone wants to start a war between Argentina and England and see Argentina win. Then they put some victorious generals they own into power and they've literally bought their own country. If someone had the millions to burn, the plan is fantastic."

"The big money to do it in South America would be drug money."

"It's a multibillion dollar industry down there."

"Bear?"

"What?"

"You're a genius."

"Thank you."

"If they're in the Antarctica, they must be near Argentina."

"I'd agree. They're probably near the Antarctic peninsula, where there is a chain of islands. They are probably posing as scientists at a research station. There are dozens of them scattered down there. They tend to huddle close to Argentina because Tierra del Fuego is close for supplies, and it's good for researchers studying Antarctic life. A good portion of the world's penguins nest there.''

''Listen, how many weapons do you think these guys could have?''

''I don't know, we're assuming it never got into production because we never heard about it. That means we're talking about working prototypes. We know they've fired six. It's possible they might have twice that many. The way you've drawn the scenario, it seems likely they're waiting for the British to come within range and then they are going to let them have it. Both sides have declared war, and the Argentine fleet is waiting off the Falklands to meet them. I don't think the Argentine captains will sit on their hands and ask questions. When the British ships start going down they'll pounce and try to clean up the survivors. It will be a blow from which England will never recover. As a nation she can't afford to replace her two carriers. England will be destroyed as a sea power. The Falkland Islands will fall to Argentina, and they will probably stay as the Islas Malvinas for the next hundred years.''

''If these guys are launching from an island in the Antarctic peninsula, I'll bet they haven't dug missile silos in the permafrost. I'm thinking they're using mobile missile launchers.'' Bolan searched his mind. ''Probably something like Russian SS-13s on tracked vehicles. That way they can roll them around the island in or out of cover, or even drive them off a cliff into the sea if they need quick denial capability.''

''I'm with you.''

''Bear, get ahold of Hal. Have him talk to the President. We need confirmation. If we can't position a satellite to hover over Antarctica, maybe we can at least get a flyby over the peninsula with some very powerful observation cameras. Tell him to authorize some SR-71 Blackbirds or something with stealth to do some high-altitude reconnaissance.''

''I'm already on it. Hal is meeting with the President and

the Joint Chiefs on the subject right now. I'll inform them of the airplane tickets to Ushuaia. That will strengthen our case."

"Good."

"What are you going to do?"

"I'm going to have a talk with Cecilia."

"I doubt whether she's going to be very cooperative."

"Maybe she won't. But I'm going to offer her the opportunity to drop a dime on her brother and bargain. Let me know as soon as we have any kind of fix on the target area."

"Will do. Striker?"

"What?"

"Stay away from her feet."

**21**

Modern United States nuclear attack submarines didn't have brigs for holding prisoners. However, a watertight storage compartment with its steel bulkheads and massive pressure door made as effective a prison cell as one could want. Cecilia Perez sat in the corner of the compartment and glared. Her left arm was in a cast from where Bolan had struck during the embassy assassination. Her right arm was in a sling across her shoulder and her upper torso was held by an immobilizing cast. Her feet were prudently shackled to a folding floor cleat.

Bolan entered the compartment. Able Seaman William Castaneda followed him with a locked and loaded M-16 rifle. Castaneda spoke both Spanish and Portuguese and had been promoted to interpreter if needed. Bolan spoke in Spanish.

"If she moves, cut her in two."

Castaneda aimed the muzzle of his weapon at Perez's midriff. The woman's black eyes never left Bolan's. If looks could have killed, Bolan would have been splattered all over the bulkheads. He examined the air mattress on the floor and switched to English. "Are you comfortable?"

The woman didn't blink.

"Are you in pain? Do you need to go to the bathroom?"

Gears seemed to switch behind her dark gaze. She replied in Portuguese-accented English. "No, not at the moment. What do you want?"

"I want you to call your brother."

She gazed at him unblinkingly. "Why would I wish to do that?"

Bolan didn't blink either. "Because if you don't, I'm going to kill him."

The dark eyes flared and hatred flared anew. "Release me at once or he'll have you all killed."

Bolan met her crazy stare and held it. "Your brother is on the Antarctic peninsula. We're repositioning a satellite to scan the area. United States supersonic observation planes are en route and will be combing every inch of the area with high-resolution infrared cameras within hours. If he hasn't surrendered before that happens he's going to be splattered all over the ice." He turned to Castaneda. "Translate that into Portuguese."

Perez snarled. "I understood!"

"Good. You have five seconds to make up your mind."

The beautiful eyes narrowed to slits. "You'll trace the communication."

"Of course we will. What difference does it make? Do you want to give your brother a chance to bargain, or do I let the bombers churn him into penguin food?"

Perez pulled her gaze away from Bolan's and stared at the cleat she was shackled to for long moments. "I'll speak with my brother."

Bolan turned to Castaneda. "Unshackle her." He locked his gaze with the woman's again and held it. "If you try to kick anyone aboard this sub I'm going to break your kneecaps."

She met his gaze unflinchingly. "I don't doubt it."

Castaneda unchained her and adjusted the shackle to give her a foot and a half of walking distance. She allowed him to help her to her feet and then shuffled forward. Bolan stooped to exit the compartment and the three of them slowly made their way to the communications room. Sailors stared in open wonder at the beautiful, chained woman in their midst. Bolan entered the communications room where Encizo was waiting with the communications officer and the captain.

"She's decided to cooperate."

Perez stood for a moment. She turned her eyes on the communications officer. The young lieutenant flinched at what he saw there. Perez's lip curled slightly as she told him what frequency to adjust the shortwave radio to.

The lieutenant began adjusting his dial. Perez glanced at Bolan. "He'll be expecting any communication on this wavelength to be in code. He'll find anything else suspicious."

Bolan's smile didn't reach his eyes. "You'll have to be convincing then."

The lieutenant looked up from his set. "We're ready."

The Executioner nodded. "Go ahead."

"This is the USS *Corpus Christi,* sending out to Waldemar Salome. Repeat, this is the USS *Corpus Christi* sending out to Waldemar Salome. Over."

Static came back over the receiver.

Bolan jerked his head at the radio. "Talk to your brother."

The lieutenant gingerly placed a headset around Perez's ears and adjusted the microphone close to her lips. "You're sending."

"Waldemar, this is Cecilia. I have been captured. Nico is dead. Everyone else at the house in Bahia has been killed. I'm aboard a United States submarine. The American is here. He wishes to speak with you."

There was more static on the receiver. A voice suddenly spoke a short phrase in Portuguese. Castaneda quickly translated. "He asked if she was all right."

Bolan nodded and put a hand on Perez's good shoulder. "Answer in English. Tell him to do the same."

"My collarbone was broken in the fighting. I have since received medical attention. I haven't been mistreated or interrogated. The American wishes to speak to you. He wishes to speak in English. They are tracing this communication."

The voice came back. "I understand. I'll speak with him."

Bolan punched the button to put the communication across the speakers.

"Surrender. Immediately."

There was a moment's pause. "No. Why don't you give me a reason?"

"Because I'll bomb the hell out of you if you don't."

"No, you won't. I might be tempted to fire all my remaining missiles at the Argentine fleet that is standing off the Falklands."

"You might be able to sink some ships. But both the Argentine and the British governments have been informed of what I have found out about you and your activities. Neither is sure if they believe it, but the British fleet is holding position, and I believe the Argentine fleet will steam north out of range any moment."

"They won't be able to sail away fast enough."

"That will be a comfort for you when the bombers blow you to hell."

Salome sighed. "I don't believe that you know exactly where I am."

"Academic. We know you're on the Antarctic peninsula. We know you are covert at a research station. There aren't that many targets to choose from. In about twenty minutes a United States observation satellite is going to fly over the area. Three more are going to join it in rapid order. We're going to see any kind of evacuation attempt you make. I'm also entertaining the idea that you have a diesel-electric submarine lying low in the area for evacuation. United States, British and Argentine submarines are all converging on your area. Any submarine detected in the area that can't transmit the correct recognition codes will be sunk immediately."

"You have thought this out very carefully."

"If your missiles are on high-launch readiness I want you to disengage them. You'll leave all other weapons inside your compound and you and your men will be out on the ice in orderly lines within twelve hours to be arrested.''

"That doesn't leave me with very much to show for my cooperation.''

"I'll make you one concession. The United States, England, Argentina, Chile and the United Nations all want you to stand trial. You have sunk ships in international waters. Well over a thousand sailors of various nations have died at your hands. You have also been responsible for the assassinations of both Argentine and British diplomats, the death of United States Marines, as well as members of the Argentine federal police. Your sister is in my custody. If you surrender, I'll release her to the United Nations or the British government. I'll even let you choose which one you want.''

"Why is this important?''

"Because neither British courts nor the United Nations war crimes tribunals currently have the death sentence.''

"Ah.''

"What is your answer?''

The voice on the intercom turned cold. "I'll tell you what. You'll take your sub due west and put in at the first port of call. You'll release my sister. When she communicates to me that she is in a safe place, I'll leave my current position. You'll make no attempt to stop me. When I believe that I'm safe, I'll deactivate my missiles and let you collect them.''

Bolan's voice grew hard. "I know that it's within your capability to launch a strike against the Argentine task force. That is the only reason I'm bargaining with you. The Argentine president has been informed of the situation. His reaction was that we should go ahead and bomb the hell out of you and let him worry about his fleet.''

"I don't doubt it.''

"Stand down and surrender. Immediately. Or you can argue with laser-guided bombs.''

"I repeat, you will release my sister. You, the British fleet and the Argentines will stand down. When my sister and I are safe, I may deactivate my missiles. If you don't, I will launch the remaining portion of my antiship weapons at the Argentine fleet standing off the Falkland Islands.''

Bolan shrugged. "You're dead.''

Perez snarled and tried to twist away. Bolan held her in place. The voice over the radio grew colder still. "Two of my ballistic missiles I will retain. Both of these missiles have thermonuclear warheads. They are aimed at Buenos Aires. As I suspect you know, Argentina has absolutely no antiballistic missile capability whatsoever. My technicians have adjusted the fuses of the warheads so that one will be an airburst and one will detonate on the ground. The results should be nothing short of spectacular.''

Bolan punched the intercom button to shut out Salome. Aaron Kurtzman had been listening by satellite link to the whole conversation. "Bear, can he do it?''

"If he has the warheads. Buenos Aires would be in range of SS-13s or any other mobile missile of Russian manufacture he might have, and the only nation in the world with any practical defense against such an attack is Russia.''

Bolan punched the intercom. "I don't believe you have the warheads.''

"I tell you what I will do. I'll have my technicians readjust the missiles' target vectors. Ninety-eight percent of the Falkland Islands' population resides in Port Stanley. I'll nuke it instead. The second missile I'll reserve for Buenos Aires. My technicians inform me that this will take approximately thirty minutes. I don't believe your bombers can reach me before I launch, and you don't even know exactly where I am yet. I'll leave the decision up to you. You may do as I ask now, or you can wait and watch what happens to Port Stanley. You may then reestablish contact with me and we will discuss Buenos Aires.''

"Salome, you'll be the most hunted man on earth.''

"I've already been dead once." The voice turned mocking. "Did you know that there's not one photograph of me in current Brazilian police records? Nor are my photographs on file anywhere. There isn't one person other than my sister who could give you an accurate description of what I look like. Those around me at the moment won't survive long after my departure. It has been arranged."

Bolan's fist clenched.

Salome's voice turned cold again. "Decide. Everyone stands down, now. All U.S., British and Argentine subs will surface and begin steaming due north. I warn you, the mobile missile launchers I have came with rather powerful defensive radars. If I detect any planes at all, I'll launch anyway, and we'll let God sort things out between us afterward. Do we have an agreement or do we speak again after I nuke the Falklands?"

Every instinct told him that Salome was speaking the truth.

Salome's voice spoke with barely concealed malice. "By the way. I'm aware of your idea of having B-2 stealth bombers fly in once you have established my position. I'll tell you now. The two nuclear-armed missiles are at a separate location. Not far, but far enough away, and concealed. Their launch sequence is on a dead man's switch. If my position is bombed and I'm killed, the missiles launch automatically."

Perez turned and her black eyes sparkled. Her smile was hideous. She spoke a single word.

"*Malicia.*"

Bolan's fist unclenched. He took a deep breath and let it out.

"We're standing down."

*Stony Man Farm, Virginia*

"Do you think the nuclear threat is a bluff?"

Hal Brognola, the director of Sensitive Operations at Stony

Man Farm, stared at the radio speaker and considered the President's question. "No, sir, I don't. Every step of the way during this crisis Salome hasn't moved without having backup and escape routes. I believe the threat is credible and I believe he's willing to carry it out."

"I have spoken with the president of Argentina. He has asked me to launch a limited nuclear ICBM strike against the Antarctic peninsula. Key members of the Pentagon agree with him, but they want to use B-2 stealth bombers. They say it's the only sure way to stop the threat."

Brognola and Bolan had already discussed this. "I disagree. It's not sure at all. Salome says his nuclear missiles are in separate locations. All he needs is a cleft in the ice or an island between his nukes and the blast and the missiles fly when he's killed and the dead man's switch goes off. The only sure thing about such an attack would be that not only would Buenos Aires and Port Stanley get nuked, but the Antarctic would be ecologically destroyed."

The President didn't sound pleased. "So, your counsel is to capitulate."

"No. If we do that, any terrorist who can get hold of a nuke will know that they can bargain for whatever they want."

"What do you recommend, then?"

"I think you should send in two stealth bombers. In one will be my men. The Russian air-defense radar Salome has won't be able to detect them, and if we jump from the bomb bay in a high-altitude, low-opening jump, his radar won't detect my men coming in. We assault his base, hopefully taking him by surprise. We secure the switch and destroy any launch capability."

"That's a mighty big if."

"It is. If we fail, or the assault stalls, we'll signal you. The second B-2 will then nuke the area. That will still have the same chance of failure as before, but at least it will give us two chances to stop Salome's nuclear strike rather than one.''

The radio was silent for a moment. Then the President of the United States spoke.

"Do it."

**22**

*Antarctic Ocean*

The *Spirit of Kittyhawk* flew steadily on. The great, bat-winged B-2 stealth bomber's four turbojet engines maintained an altitude of thirty-eight thousand feet and a cruising speed of 580 miles per hour. Behind the leader, the *Spirit of Texas* followed in a loose formation. Mack Bolan sat in a small pressurized compartment just aft of the *Kittyhawk*'s flight deck. The small compartment was crowded with the five men and their weapons and equipment. The rest of the team, like sensible soldiers, were asleep. But the Executioner was in command. He stayed awake.

Bolan didn't like this mission. He and his men were going to make a high-altitude, low-opening jump. All of his team had made HALO jumps before, but most of them had never jumped from a B-2. The disturbance in the air as it flowed over the B-2 at two hundred miles per hour would be bad. It would be like dropping into a hurricane. And they were jumping heavy. Each man had an M-4 Ranger carbine in a jump case, except for Encizo, who carried a .50 caliber Barret sniper rifle. All of them were festooned with spare magazines, grenades, assorted knives and pistols.

Jumping with all that gear wasn't the safest thing in the world, much less landing in Antarctica at night, but Bolan had decided they must take the risk. No one knew what the situation was on the island. He and his men had to be ready to fight the moment they hit the ground. There was one other thing to worry about. The plane flying behind them was carrying a nuclear payload. If Bolan and his team failed, they wouldn't survive plan B. A voice suddenly spoke in Bolan's earpiece. He recognized the copilot's voice on the intercom.

"Major Eishen says we're fifteen minutes out. You and your men should get ready to jump."

"Roger. Will comply," Bolan answered and started rousing his team. The next ten minutes were hectic as the men struggled into their helmets, chutes and gear. Some strong opinions were expressed about whoever had designed the B-2's cramped and awkward weapons bay, but Bolan's men were old hands, and somehow they got it done. Bolan checked each man's oxygen tanks and mask personally. At thirty-eight thousand feet, the outside air was so thin that anyone whose mask or tanks failed would be unconscious in thirty seconds. Bolan finished his check. He and his men were ready.

The one-minute warning light was on. The bomb bay was no longer pressurized. Bolan and his men were breathing oxygen from their bail-out bottles, the individual oxygen tanks that would keep them alive until they were below ten thousand feet. Bolan was acting as his own jump master. He gave each man a final check. Their faces and heads were covered by their helmets and masks. Gloves, boots, masks and insulated jumpsuits protected the rest of their bodies. It was seventy degrees below zero outside.

Bolan made a thumbs-up gesture at his men. Each man returned the gesture. No one was having breathing problems or trouble with his gear. Bolan pointed upward, and each man gripped the nylon drop net. They were spaced around the outer edges of the net. When it was released, the heavily weighted center would pull them down rapidly through the air flow around the B-2's huge body.

The thirty-second warning light came on. There was a sudden change in the roar of the engines as the pilot throttled back. He would hold the big bomber as close to stalling speed as he could in order to minimize the airflow. When he was satisfied, he would push the ten-second warning light. That would activate the drop sequence. Unless Bolan called an abort, they would go.

The *Spirit of Kittyhawk* began to shudder and shake as her speed dropped to within a few knots of stalling. Satisfied, her pilot pushed the button. The ten-second light came on as the last warning before the jump. The bomb-bay doors swung smoothly open beneath their boots and Bolan's stomach dropped as his arms took the strain. He and his team were hanging from the drop net with nothing beneath them.

Bolan looked down and saw a god's eye view of Deception Island in the flat green and gray of his night-vision goggles. Air shrieked and howled through the open doors. The go light went on. There was a loud cracking noise as the tiny explosive devices cut the drop net free. The weighted center of the net dropped instantly through the doors. Bolan and his team were buffeted by the airstream as the net pulled them down and clear. Bolan spoke into the mike in his mask.

"Three! Two! One! Release!" The net dropped away. Bolan and his men were in free fall. Looking up, Bolan could see the giant shape of the *Spirit of Kittyhawk* as she pulled away. Her aft bomb-bay doors were open and cargo drop containers were falling into the slipstream.

Bolan used his arms and legs to assume a facedown position. He was counting to himself without thinking as he glanced quickly to the left and right. At the moment, things were almost peaceful. The air was clear and brilliant with stars. The roar of the B-2 engines faded into silence. All Bolan could hear was the sound of his demand-regulated breathing and the air sighing as he fell through space. Looking down, he could see the island below him. He could see the lumps of sheds and buildings. No perimeter lights were visible. Salome was maintaining a blackout in his compound. Bolan looked out toward the shore of the island and could just make out the shapes of the SS-13 launchers. He counted twelve of them. Six of them appeared to be empty of missiles. He scanned the perimeter of the island but he couldn't see the two launchers that supposedly had the nuclear-tipped weapons.

Bolan glanced at the altimeter on his wrist. He was at eight thousand feet now. He unsnapped his oxygen mask. He could feel the frigid air against his face. There was little or no low-altitude wind. Good. The critical thing was to get his men down together and ready to fight before the enemy could react, if they had been detected.

He checked his altimeter again, five thousand feet. He could see the landing zone to his left. The ground seemed to rush up toward him faster and faster. Bolan put his hand on the *D* ring. Even through his glove the feel of the cold metal was reassuring, but he wouldn't pull the rip cord until he hit five hundred feet. The low-altitude opening would minimize the chances of detection no matter what warning systems the people on the ground were using.

He glanced at his altimeter again, one thousand feet. Things began happening very fast. The flat ice of the landing zone was now rushing at him. At five hundred feet Bolan pulled his rip cord. His pilot chute deployed, pulling his special high-performance, ram-air canopy out of its pack and into the air. The canopy blossomed, and Bolan felt a strong jolt as it filled with air and slowed his fall. Quickly, he slipped his hands into his steering loops, ready to maneuver if he had to. A collision with one of his men could scrub the mission, and they would all fry in the nuclear fireball as the unseen *Spirit of Texas* exercised the final option. Rapidly, he looked around and counted, one, two, three, four. He felt a surge of relief. Everyone's chute had opened. He estimated the dispersion of his group at less than one hundred meters. Their special chutes could be flown like hang gliders. They should be able to come down close together on the assembly point. He pulled on his steering loops and went to full brake. Bolan lost all forward thrust from his canopy, and hung on the edge of a stall. As he lost forward motion, his rate of descent increased. The landing zone was directly below him. He went to half brake and turned to the right. He completed his turn and went to full brake. He was falling straight down.

Bolan pulled the release and felt his equipment pack drop away and dangle below him. Deception Island lurched up to meet him. Bolan hit hard and his boots slid on unyielding ice. He rolled with bone-jarring force and came to his feet. He felt a thrill of relief. He was down and safe. Bolan pulled his quick-release handles and slipped out of his parachute harness.

The rest of the men descended in tight formation. Bolan tensed as one of his men landed hard. The goggled and insulated figure twisted as he hit and rolled badly across the ice. Gary Manning's voice came across the radio in a snarl. "Goddamn it!"

Bolan rushed to the big Canadian's side. "Gary! You all right?"

Manning rose to his feet and promptly fell back down again as he put weight on his right leg. The lenses of the night vision goggles looked up at Bolan. Manning's lips twisted in self-reproach beneath his mask. "I've done something to my ankle."

"What kind of something?"

Encizo, Grimaldi and McCarter faced outward looking for movement. The tip of Manning's boot twitched experimentally and his breath came in a hiss. "It's busted."

Bolan's face tightened. With Schwarz out with a concussion, Manning had been brought in to fill the gap. Now Bolan was down to four men again. McCarter spoke quietly. "We can carry him to the other side of the island. That would put some big rock formations between us and the blast, and we can dig an ice shelter. We might just be able to weather it out.''

It was an ugly option. Water would absorb radiation, and ice was frozen water, but the only tools they had for the job were their fighting knives and they would have to try to build a shelter out of sheet ice and frozen rock. Bolan smiled grimly. ''I don't think an antiradiation igloo is an option at the moment.''

McCarter shrugged. ''So we go in with four.''

Manning looked up from his ankle. ''Tell you what, give me Rafe's rifle. I'll crawl toward the shore and find a decent position. If any of the missiles go hot, I'll put a few armor-piercing incendiaries into them.''

Bolan nodded. Encizo gave Manning the gigantic Barret rifle. Manning levered himself to his good foot and took the weapon by the barrel. Without a word he began hobbling toward the beach on his .50-caliber crutch. Bolan nodded toward the compound. ''Let's move.''

Bolan, McCarter, Encizo and Grimaldi moved out across the ice.

Bolan moved toward the darkened compound. It looked like more than the average research station. There were too many buildings and a concrete bunker that just didn't belong in Antarctica as a seasonal facility devoted to studying penguins.

The night-vision goggles Bolan wore didn't detect heat, instead they magnified the ambient light present. This amplification took the Antarctic starlight and intensified it. He paused. The ghostly beams of infrared detection lasers crisscrossed around the camp's perimeter at knee level. Such beams would be invisible to the naked eye, but anyone breaking the beam would set off an alarm in the command shack. Bolan knelt and felt the ground. Where there was no ice there was rock, and where there was earth it was permafrost and felt hard as iron. Bolan doubted very much whether Salome would have taken the time and expended the resources to place magnetic or motion detectors in the ground.

Bolan stayed in his crouch. Rocks and obstructions had been cleared in the compound area in all directions. Bolan examined the grounds. There were a number of prefab buildings. The observation tower rose over the camp. There were two warehouse-like structures, and the bunker, shaped like a cross of concrete.

Bolan made his choice. The windows of the bunker faced outward toward the missiles near the beach, and unlike the prefab huts, he could probably climb on top of the cement bunker without alerting the occupants. There were also aerial antennae and a dish he could take a stab at hiding behind to avoid being seen by the people in the tower. However, the camp had to be on a high state of alert. Someone had to be watching the compound area, possibly with cameras from within the bunker, and someone else had to be monitoring the early-warning radar and the camp's own security suite.

"I'm going to try to get on top of the command bunker. Everyone else hold position."

"Roger that."

Bolan began moving toward the camp. He stopped at the last clump of rocks available for cover.

"Gary, how are you doing?"

Gary Manning's voice responded wearily. "I'm in position. Confirm twelve SS-13 tracked launch vehicles. Six missile launchers are empty. Six more are loaded and elevated on their rails. I've got a good line of fire on all six from my position. You give me the word and I'll start punching holes in their rocket motors."

"Hold your position. Fire only if instructed or if the rocket motors start to fire."

"Roger that. I also have a small concrete bunker down here in the rocks. I could see a cigarette glow through the observation slit. The bunker looks out on the beach and the missiles. I can try crawling up on it and taking them out quietly or asking them some questions."

Bolan thought fast. Anyone in the bunker was probably a guard. They wouldn't have the capability to fire the missiles. They were there to warn the main camp if Navy SEALs came sneaking up the beach toward the weapons.

"Hold position."

"Holding."

"Rafe, what do you have in the guard tower?"

Along with the rest of his load, Encizo carried high-powered, night-vision, laser-range-finding binoculars.

"I make two hostiles in the tower shed. Both have binoculars. They must have night-vision capability. Russian make by the shape but I won't swear to it. They're taking turns scanning the perimeter."

Bolan's raidsuit and parka were painted in the U.S. army's night-vision disruptive pattern, and had been insulated and treated to prevent his heat signature from revealing him to infrared detectors. Behind his clump of rocks, small as it was, he was still invisible. Once inside the camp's fire zone he would be perilously exposed, and if the camp was alerted, Bolan knew it would light up like a Christmas tree and he would be cut down by riflemen firing out of the buildings. It would have to be a 150-yard sprint to the bunker or nothing.

"Rafe, tell me when no one is looking this way."

"Roger that. Hold tight."

Bolan slung his carbine and grenade launcher and drew his 9 mm Beretta pistol with attached sound suppressor. He centered his mind and relaxed as he waited. He didn't look directly at the tower or the bunker. He kept his eye on the infrared beam of light that hovered at knee level at the camp's perimeter.

"Move! Move! Move!"

Bolan vaulted the rocks and hit the ground at a dead run.

His feet sounded incredibly loud as they pounded the ice and rock but Bolan knew the camp was shut tight against the cold. It was the eyes in the tower he had to worry about, and the eyes he didn't know about.

The soldier hurdled the infrared laser beam and ran through the death zone surrounding the camp. Brief thoughts of motion detectors and mines flashed through his mind. Bolan crushed the thoughts and sprinted at the bunker.

Deception Island was all slick rock and ice, and the soles of Bolan's boots were soft rubber to grip it. The ball of his right foot hit the concrete wall. Bolan leaped upward and caught the rough edge of the bunker. He swung his leg up and rolled flat onto the roof. The soldier rolled onto his hands and knees and quickly put the satellite dish between himself and the observation tower.

Encizo spoke in his ear. "No movement. I detect no apparent reaction. The men in the tower were facing each other and talking while you ran."

Bolan crouched in place and let his breathing return to normal. He was above the side door of the bunker. The door was made of heavy steel set into the concrete. Blowing the door was not an option. If Salome really had a dead man's switch on the missiles, blowing the door or even trying to blow the whole bunker could well spell disaster.

Bolan folded himself into a half-lotus position behind the satellite dish, tucked his parka closer around his face and waited. Time passed very slowly. It was 3:15 in the morning.

At 3:45 a.m. the door below him clanked as its bolts were unlocked.

Bolan unfolded his legs and resumed his crouch. Light spilled out onto the frozen ground as the door opened and then shut again. A man stood below him with his back to the bunker. The man fumbled in his jacket and a second later Bolan heard the unmistakable chinking noise of a Zippo lighter flicking open. A moment later the soldier breathed in the powerful smell of a Cuban cigar.

Encizo spoke in Bolan's earpiece without being asked. "Hold position, Striker, the guards in the tower are watching your target."

Bolan waited behind his cover. The man sighed and let out a long drag of smoke from his cigar. It was intensely cold outside, but Bolan could well imagine how claustrophobic it must be inside the command bunker. The man would take some time to savor his cigar.

"You're clear! No one's looking!"

Bolan cocked his fist behind his head and leaped.

Bolan's fist swung in an arc as he fell, crashing into the side of the man's head. The man was swatted to the ground and Bolan fell into a crouch beside him. He seized the man by the throat but there was no reaction. He was unconscious. Bolan yanked him into a fireman's carry and ran around the side of the bunker. Bolan dashed for the deeper blackness of the shadows and dumped his prisoner.

Encizo watched over him like a guardian angel. "No movement. No reaction. Clear so far."

Bolan turned his prisoner over and his palm cracked against his cheek like a gunshot. The man jerked and his eyes flew open. The Executioner clamped his palm over the man's mouth and pressed the muzzle of the Beretta between his eyes. He spoke in Spanish. "Who are you?"

He lifted his hand slightly and the man stared up at him in confused terror. Bolan repeated himself and the man blinked in horror. Spanish was close enough to Portuguese that the question should have been fairly clear. On a hunch Bolan switched to Russian.

"Quietly. What is your name?"

The man tensed with the change of language. Bolan pressed the Beretta harder on his forehead. The man whispered rapidly. "Rabovskya! My name is Rabovskya!"

"You're one of the engineers?"

"I'm a missile technician."

"Where are the nukes?"

The man's face tightened. Bolan screwed the muzzle of the Beretta against Rabovskya's brow. "Answer right now or I'll kill you and ask the next man who leaves the bunker. Lie to me, and I order a nuclear strike on this island. We'll all die."

"You wouldn't dare!"

Bolan flicked the Beretta selector lever from semiauto to 3-round burst mode.

"An island! South of here!"

"Coordinates!"

"Latitude 62.5748 degrees south. Longitude 60.3825 degrees west!"

"How are they concealed?"

"Two shallow prefabricated domes. Fifty yards apart. They barely fit over the launchers. They are camouflaged and look like snow mounds. On the launch sequence the charges fire and the missiles elevate and then launch."

"What kind of crew?"

"Three men at each dome."

"How are they armed?"

"I don't know."

Bolan leaned on the grips of the Beretta. "How are they armed? Do they have shoulder-launched anti-aircraft missiles? Cannons?"

"I don't know!"

"What are the targets?"

"Buenos Aires and Port Stanley!"

Bolan eased the pressure on the Russian's skull slightly. Everything Salome had promised was now confirmed. The threat was real. Millions of lives were at stake. The Falkland Islands would be reduced to radioactive rocks. There were also still six more loaded SS-13 launchers on the beach holding over a thousand Argentine sailors hostage.

It was time to end Salome's game. "How are you evacuating?"

"We are expecting a submarine anytime now."

Bolan hog-tied Rabovskya and taped his mouth shut. "Rafe."

"Right here."

"Tie me in to *Spirit of Texas*."

Bolan waited a moment as Encizo patched through the frequency. Major Michelle Westladen's voice came back. "This is *Spirit of Texas*, Striker."

"I have a probable location on the nuclear missiles. An island, due south, coordinates, latitude, 62.5748 degrees south, longitude, 60.3825 degrees west. They are concealed to look like snow mounds. Fifty yards apart."

"What is the anti-aircraft environment?"

"Unknown, automatic rifles at least."

There was a moment of silence on the line. "I'm going to have to go in low. They are probably going to hear my engines. After that things are going to start happening fast."

"Affirmative, I'm holding position."

Encizo's voice spoke urgently. "Striker! Hostiles leaving the bunker!"

A voice shouted out from the front of the bunker. "Rabovskya!"

Rabovskya tensed beneath Bolan's knee. The voice shouted again. "Rabovskya!"

Bolan shouted back. "What?" He rose and began walking around the corner of the building.

The voice shouted back angrily. "What the hell are you doing out here?"

Bolan came around the corner. Two men stood, waiting. One carried an AK-47 rifle slung across his back. Bolan put three quick rounds into the rifleman's chest and turned the Beretta on the other. The man yanked at something in his parka. The Executioner squeezed the Beretta's trigger and hammered him down. He snarled into his throat mike as he holstered the pistol and whipped his carbine around on its sling.

"Everyone! Move in!"

The bunker door was open and Bolan had no time to wait for backup. Salome had to have a bolt-hole. Bolan couldn't wait and play hide and seek on the island while Salome slipped away on a submarine. The soldier pulled a frag grenade from his belt and pulled the pin. The cotter pin pinged away as he released the safety lever. Bolan tossed the grenade through the open bunker door and stepped aside.

Beyond the perimeter Encizo's grenade launcher boomed. A second later, glass shattered in the guard tower and white phosphorus bloomed into lurid white fire. McCarter and Grimaldi came charging across the fire zone of the camp.

The camp suddenly lit up as floodlights blazed.

Major Westladen's voice spoke urgently in Bolan's ear from the cockpit of the *Spirit of Texas*. "I have small heat signatures flashing on the target area. Four flares. Fifty yards apart."

They could only be one thing. The charges that tore away the nuclear weapon's camouflaged domes had been fired. The nukes were launching.

"Take them out!"

"Affirmitive, Striker! Am closing to attack!" The B-2 stealth bomber had two weapons bays. One held the nuclear payload Bolan didn't want to think about. The other carried eight two-thousand pound laser-guided bombs. "Two silos! Tracked vehicles, elevating missiles to launch position! Allocating two weapons to each silo! Laser designators locked! Closing in! Bombs away!"

Bolan called out to Manning across the radio. "Gary! Take out those missiles! Now!"

"Affirmative!" From the northern beach the report of

Manning's .50 caliber sniper rifle began hammering in rapid semiautomatic fire.

Bolan stepped away from the door as green tracers streaked out of it and the thunder of a heavy machine gun echoed in the bunker. "Rafe, Jack, David! Fall back!"

The three men scattered and fell back into the darkness outside the perimeter of the camp. Men began spilling out of the barracks with rifles in their hands. Bolan pulled a fade around the edge of the bunker. The men's heads whipped south as thunder clapped in the cloudless sky and orange fire lit up the horizon to the south. Explosion after explosion echoed and rolled.

"Striker! This is Westladen. Both launchers destroyed! Repeat, both launchers destroyed!"

Gary Manning's voice cut in sharply. "Missiles launching on the beach! Rocket motors are firing! Am maintaining fire!"

It was time to cross fingers. The SS-13s had solid propellant rocket motors rather than liquid fuel. Manning was shooting them with armor-piercing incendiary ammunition. The missiles wouldn't simply ignite like gasoline. The .50 caliber bullets would punch into the solid fuel cells and begin burning.

"Striker! Missile away!"

Bolan watched as the SS-13 rose from the beach on a column of flame. There was something wrong with the missile. A jet of orange fire shot out from its side and began to push it slightly off its line of ascent. The jet grew bigger and bigger as the burning rocket fuel ate the hole in its side larger. The missile began to yaw through the air. Without warning its rocket motor exploded and detonated its antiship warhead.

Orange fire lit up the Antarctic night. Another missile rose off its rails and fire jetted out of its side in three different directions. It twisted crazily into the night and arced off west rather than north toward the Falklands. A third missile rose and blew up almost immediately.

The island rumbled as one of the SS-13s blew up on its launcher. Burning rocket fuel flew in all directions and was driven by the explosion of the high-explosive warhead. The remaining three SS-13s blew up like massive firecrackers.

Salome's riflemen were pouring out the barracks. Some carried submachine guns and by the way they sprayed their weapons into the darkness it was obvious they were street criminals. The majority ran out with their AK-47s at the hip assault position like Russian ex-military personnel. Salome had brought in some real muscle.

Bolan faded back into the darkness. "Westladen, this is Striker, over."

"This is Westladen. What can we do for you?"

"I've got riflemen coming out in platoon strength. I've got three men and I need help convincing them to surrender."

"Affirmative, Striker. I'm inbound, ETA three minutes. What is my target?"

"Deploy one weapon on the command bunker. Cross-shaped structure, directly south of the observation tower. Observation tower is on fire. You can't miss it."

"Affirmative. Clear your team."

Bolan broke into a run outside the camp's killing zone. He leaped for a clump of rocks as tracers streaked overhead and bullets ricocheted off the rocks. He flipped up the sight of his grenade launcher, then pulled the trigger and the white phosphorus grenade arced high like a mortar round to blossom into fire in the middle of the camp.

The rock he leaned on shuddered and vibrated as something heavier than a rifle struck it. The Russians were bringing out heavier weapons. Bolan jacked another grenade into his launcher. They were expecting a submarine. They couldn't allow themselves to be pinned down in the command bunker. At any cost they were going to break out and try to meet it.

But Bolan was in their way.

"Jack! What's your situation?"

"We're pinned down, Striker! We have cover but we are taking heavy fire." There was a split second pause. "Striker! They are coming right at you!"

"Striker! This is Westladen. Bunker designated!"

"I'm 150 yards west of the bunker! Drop the artillery between me and it. I'm firing my weapon! Mark my position!"

Bolan fired his grenade launcher. On the flat plain of the island the B-2's infrared camera would see the muzzle blast of the M-203 as a bright flash.

"We see you, Striker! Hold on!"

The stealth bomber was coming in low. The roar of its engines rumbled above the sound of automatic fire. Bolan looked up and a great shadow blotted out the stars as the B-2 came in. Gunmen turned and raised their rifles to fire at it. Bolan curled himself into a ball behind his rocks and covered his ears. No rockets or missiles fired from the great bomber. It simply seemed to roar overhead. The air shook as it flew over. No one saw or heard the laser-guided bomb deploy.

The earth shuddered. Bolan squeezed his eyes shut and still saw orange light behind his eyelids. The blast wave rolled over his cover in a wash of pressure and heat.

The voice in his earpiece seemed to speak to him from underwater. "Striker, perimeter is clear! All targets down!"

Bolan had no doubt. Charging men without cover stood no chance against a laser-guided bomb. Those who hadn't been blown to bits had been flung like rag dolls. The survivors wouldn't be in any shape to do anything. But there were still others to deal with.

"Westladen, deploy second weapon! Take out the bunker!"

"Affirmative, Striker!"

Bolan stayed where he was and waited while Major Westladen completed her turn. He peered over his cover at the compound. Most of the lights had been blown out by the blast. The observation tower leaned perilously to one side and burned like a torch in the night. Bodies were strewn everywhere and there was a great crater between him and the compound. Fires burned out beyond the beach where Manning had destroyed the remaining SS-13s.

"*Kittyhawk!* This is Striker! What do you see?"

Major Eishen's voice came over the radio. *Kittyhawk* had stayed at high altitude to observe. "No movement, Striker."

Bolan hunkered back down and waited for *Spirit of Texas* to make her strike. Her engines vibrated the air. Salome wouldn't have come out with the initial counterattack.

He would have an escape hole.

"Striker! Weapon away!"

Bolan braced himself. The blast was seventy-five yards away and he felt much less of the shock, but Bolan stayed down. Seconds later, chunks of concrete and debris from the shattered bunker came raining out of the starry night.

Bolan rose into a crouch and surveyed the compound. The burning observation tower had been toppled by the second blast and lay broken and burning on its side. The bunker had been shattered. The prefabricated huts were battered but standing. Bolan roared out in Russian and then Spanish.

"Throw down your weapons! Come out, or the bombing continues!"

For a moment nothing moved. A door to one of the barracks opened and a rifle flew out and clattered to the ground. A man came out holding up his hands. He called out in Spanish. "Don't shoot!"

There was another pause while people waited to see if he was shot. As he stood unharmed more weapons were tossed out and men began filing out into the center of the compound.

Bolan shouted out. "On your knees! Hands over your heads!"

Men dropped and obeyed.

Bolan watched the surrender. He had no doubt in his mind. Salome wasn't coming out. He wasn't here. After the first blast he had made his move.

"Striker, this is *Kittyhawk*. I have a submarine running on the surface two miles from the island, due north. I have no reports of friendlies in the area. It isn't emitting the recognition signal."

"Affirmative. Designate a bomb but don't deploy yet."

"Affirmative, Striker."

Due north would be coming straight toward the beach where the missiles were. Most people would have dug the tunnel away from the likely line of attack. A tunnel due north would exit right where a strike force of SEALs would have hit the beach to attack the launchers. It would allow him to pop up behind his attackers. Perez's words on the *Corpus Christi*'s secure communication room rang in Bolan's mind.

"*Malicia.*" Knowing what an opponent is going to do and defeating him before he makes his move.

"Jack, Rafe, David, what do you have?"

"No movement, Striker."

"Gary, what's the situation on the beach?"

There was no reply. "Gary, come in."

Nothing came back. "Everyone hold position, keep the prisoners down, we don't want them rearming themselves."

Bolan moved out at a run down the beach. He veered wide to flank from the east. He slowed as he approached. The fires from the burning missile launcher lit everything in orange and red shadows. Bolan rose and moved to his next cover.

Gunfire rang out.

Bolan twisted as the bullet struck him in the chest. The gun fired again and again. Sparks flew from his carbine and the weapon shuddered and twisted in his hands. More bullets hit him and Bolan flung himself behind a ridge of low rocks. They barely covered him and left him with no room to fire back or maneuver. Suddenly, the gunfire ceased. Bolan ran his hands over his weapon. The grenade launcher had been perforated, and the forestock of his rifle was dented and torn.

A voice spoke in accented English. "Hey, man, are you still alive?"

Bolan eased his Desert Eagle from its holster.

"Maybe I'll just shoot your friend here if you don't answer."

Bolan loosened the Beretta in its holster for a quick draw. "I'm alive."

"Why don't you toss out your pistols and come out?"

"Why don't you surrender while you have the chance?"

"I'm going to count to three then blow your friend's head off." The voice addressed Manning. "Say something to your friend."

Gary Manning spoke in grim embarrassment. "He snuck up on me. My leg kept me from doing anything about it."

Salome spoke. "Stand and toss away your pistols. I'm not going to kill you. I need you to issue some orders, but I don't trust you behind that rock. You might get some idea of trying something stupid."

A plan began to form in Bolan's mind. He tossed out the Desert Eagle.

"All of them."

Bolan tossed out the Beretta.

"The rest of them."

Bolan grimaced. His plan had just become infinitely more difficult. He unsnapped the little Centennial revolver and tossed it away.

"Stand."

Bolan stood slowly. Salome was forty yards away. Manning was sprawled out unhappily at his feet. Salome pointed a large automatic pistol at Manning's head.

"Drop your grenade belt."

Bolan unhooked the web belt and let it fall. Salome nodded. "Good. Now, order the bombers to withdraw. Order your men at the compound to surrender to the men they are holding."

Bolan was silent. Salome shrugged. "Do it, or I'll shoot your friend. If you still refuse, I'll shoot you. Don't doubt me."

The soldier had no doubts. When the attack had begun, Salome had ordered a nuclear strike against the entire civilian population of Buenos Aires. Bolan took half a step forward. Salome raised his pistol and aimed it at Bolan's head. "Give the order, now!"

Bolan gave the order into his throat mike. "*Texas*, deploy."

For long seconds nothing happened. Salome snarled. "Give the order, I want to—"

Thunder erupted out on the water. The horizon lit up as the bomb struck the submarine and detonated. Salome jumped and his head whipped around.

Bolan surged into a dead sprint. His Ka-bar knife slid from its sheath. Salome recovered and whipped his pistol in line with Bolan.

Gary Manning swung his forearm and chopped Salome at the back of his knees. Salome's legs swung out from under him. His feet rose and his right foot effortlessly slammed into Manning's jaw. He continued into a back handspring. Salome landed on his feet with the power and grace of an Olympic gymnast. He came up with his pistol leveled.

Bolan was less than ten yards away as he flung his fighting knife.

The blade was a sliver of silver as it revolved through the air. Salome leaned away and the weapon whirled past. Bolan dived into a shoulder roll as the pistol barked. The bullet cracked at supersonic speed where his head had been. As Bolan rolled, his hand clawed at his left ankle. His fingers closed around the steel handle of his boot knife. Bolan came up and thrust.

Salome fired again. The bullet smashed into Bolan's chest and hammered the ceramic trauma plate of his body armor. A second bullet hammered him, but the armor held.

The five-inch blade sank through Salome's parka. The Executioner took another hammer blow to the chest and ripped his knife upward. Salome snarled and the muzzle of his pistol scraped up from Bolan's chest as he tried to point it at Bolan's head. The soldier jerked his head aside and the world exploded in the muzzle-blast and flame of the pistol going off beside his skull.

Bolan yanked the knife free and rammed it up under Salome's jaw. He ripped the knife across and Salome stiffened as his carotids were cut. Waldemar Salome fell facedown to the stones and didn't move.

Bolan scooped up the fallen handgun and scanned the area as he walked over to Manning.

"Gary, are you all right?"

Manning had sat up and was rubbing his jaw. "Now I know how Gadgets felt."

Bolan adjusted his earpiece. "This is Striker. Send out the message. We have taken the island. All missiles destroyed. Salome is dead. We have at least twenty prisoners. I have one injured man. We need immediate backup and evacuation."

Major Westladen's voice came over the earpiece. "Affirmative, Striker. Sending."

Bolan looked down at Manning. "If I give you an arm, can you hobble?"

"My head is fine, it's the leg that hurts like hell."

Bolan smiled in the light of the burning missile launchers. "Those were Russians back at the compound. They're bound to have some vodka lying around."

Manning grinned as he clasped Bolan's wrist and heaved himself up. "I'll race you."

# James Axler

# OUTLANDERS™

## WREATH OF FIRE

Ambika, an amazon female, has been gathering groups of
Outlanders in the Western Isles in an attempt to overthrow
the Barons. But are her motives just a ploy to satisfy her
own ambition?

A nuclear threat...

# STONY MAN™ 45

# STAR VENTURE

Red Chinese agents hijack an American state-of-the-art spaceship and use it to take nuclear-missile-firing platforms into space. Part of the Stony Man team goes into orbit and destroys the platforms, while the rest of the team travels to China to reclaim the spaceship.

On sale February 2000 at your favorite retail outlet.

---

# JAMES AXLER

# DEATH LANDS®

## Shadow World

Ryan Cawdor must face the threat of invaders that arrive from a parallel earth where the nukecaust never happened. And when he is abducted through a time corridor, he discovers a nightmare that makes Deathlands look tame by comparison!

On sale March 2000 at your favorite retail outlet. Or order your copy now by sending your name, address, zip or postal code, along with a check or money order (please do not send cash) for $5.99 for each book ordered ($6.99 in Canada), plus 75¢ postage and handling ($1.00 in Canada), payable to Gold Eagle Books, to:

| In the U.S. | In Canada |
|---|---|
| Gold Eagle Books | Gold Eagle Books |
| 3010 Walden Ave. | P.O. Box 636 |
| P.O. Box 9077 | Fort Erie, Ontario |
| Buffalo, NY 14269-9077 | L2A 5X3 |

Please specify book title with order.
Canadian residents add applicable federal and provincial taxes.

GDL49

# Shadow THE EXECUTIONER®
## as he battles evil for 352 pages of heart-stopping action!

## SuperBolan®

| | | | |
|---|---|---|---|
| #61452 | DAY OF THE VULTURE | $5.50 U.S.<br>$6.50 CAN. | ☐<br>☐ |
| #61453 | FLAMES OF WRATH | $5.50 U.S.<br>$6.50 CAN. | ☐<br>☐ |
| #61454 | HIGH AGGRESSION | $5.50 U.S.<br>$6.50 CAN. | ☐<br>☐ |
| #61455 | CODE OF BUSHIDO | $5.50 U.S.<br>$6.50 CAN. | ☐<br>☐ |
| #61456 | TERROR SPIN | $5.50 U.S.<br>$6.50 CAN. | ☐<br>☐ |

**(limited quantities available on certain titles)**

| | |
|---|---|
| **TOTAL AMOUNT** | $ |
| **POSTAGE & HANDLING** | $ |
| ($1.00 for one book, 50¢ for each additional) | |
| **APPLICABLE TAXES*** | $ _____ |
| **TOTAL PAYABLE** | $ _____ |
| (check or money order—please do not send cash) | |

To order, complete this form and send it, along with a check or money order for the total above, payable to Gold Eagle Books, to: **In the U.S.:** 3010 Walden Avenue, P.O. Box 9077, Buffalo, NY 14269-9077; **In Canada:** P.O. Box 636, Fort Erie, Ontario, L2A 5X3.

Name: _____

Address: _____ City: _____

State/Prov.: _____ Zip/Postal Code: _____

*New York residents remit applicable sales taxes.
 Canadian residents remit applicable GST and provincial taxes.

GSBBACK1